Tie Me Up

A Binding Collection of Erotic Tales

Edited by F. Leonora Solomon

For more information contact:
Riverdale Avenue Books
5676 Riverdale Avenue
Riverdale, NY 10471.

www.riverdaleavebooks.com

Design by www.formatting4U.com
Cover by Insatiable Fantasy Designs Inc.

Digital ISBN 9781626011748
Print ISBN 9781626011755

First Edition April 2015

Table of Contents

Introduction
By F. Leonora Solomon

I am not a novice as an editor of anthologies, far from it. But when I finished the completed manuscript of *Tie Me Up*, I felt such a sense of accomplishment and pride that was unrivaled from anything I had felt before. This is my first anthology with Riverdale Avenue Books, and I am over the moon to have this anthology published with them.

Tie Me Up, as I told people when I was editing it, is exactly what it sounds like in terms of erotica. But do not believe for one second that it is your typical bondage anthology. It is not. It is a very sexy book as the genre demands, but it is also smart and filled with surprises. It is soft-core and hardcore at the same time. I had the pleasure of working with authors that I worked with before, and authors I worked with for the first time. Every story in this book stirred something in me, and I can promise you it will stir something in you.

BDSM is the fetish du jour these days for many reasons, but especially because of *that book* which is mentioned often within these pages, because it is inevitable. But what I want you to take away from reading this anthology, aside from being aroused more than you ever thought possible, is to realize that bondage can be many things. It is not just the ideas that you conjure in your head of people tied up or suspended in the air. Bondage like any sexual activity between consenting partners and can be a more than fulfilling exchange that connects them in ways they were not expecting. There are a lot of revelations uncovered in this anthology where people are transformed. Any good sexual act or reading activity should take you to the next level. I hope *Tie Me Up* will take you to that level...

F. Leonora Solomon
New York City, 2015

Knock Three Times
By Tabitha Kitten

I needed a new lover. In fact, I needed a perfect lover. After several months of being single, I realized that I wanted someone in my life and, more importantly, in my bed. However, finding a new man was proving to be difficult. I didn't wish to hang around bars or clubs late at night, my friends were all married and there were no unattached men where I worked. So, I turned to internet dating.

But after several fruitless months of exchanging messages and meeting up with unsuitable men, I decided I needed a new approach. I made the decision that I would not ask for any personal details or photographs of the men I corresponded with. Instead, I would limit myself to the constraints of the written word and begin to build a rapport with as many eligible suitors as I pleased. I eliminated those I did not feel I would be compatible until, finally, I narrowed it down to the two potential lovers with whom I felt I shared the best connection.

My kinky plan was to then invite each of these two men to visit me in a hotel room, where I would be blindfolded so that I could not make any judgments about their physical appearance. They would be allowed to bind me, and do as they pleased for exactly one hour. The one who satisfied me the most, would become my new full-time lover.

I wrote to many men, upfront about my naughty plan and lascivious intentions. That in itself weeded out those for whom this was a step too far. But I needed the excitement, and sharing the edgy thrill of my plan would ensure that my co-conspirator was of a similar mindset and willing to fulfill my dirty little fantasy. Surprisingly – or not – most found my proposal extremely exciting. I exchanged messages and e-mails with a dozen of them and, finally, I had determined the two men would I would invite to the hotel room. On paper they were witty, intelligent and charming. I looked forward to meeting them although, of course, I wouldn't get to see them properly until after I had discovered what they could do.

***

Nervously, I sat on the bed awaiting Carl. I wore a black negligee that tied with ribbon at the neck. It was sheer, so my breasts and hard nipples could be seen through the flimsy material. I had on black stockings but decided not to wear panties, leaving my shaven pussy on display. My blonde hair was curled into loose corkscrews and I wore light make-up. Perched on top of my head was a flight eye mask at the ready.

I set the timer on my phone for exactly one hour, and waited. Minutes later, I jumped at the sound of somebody knocking three times on the door. I switched the timer to start, and walked across the room. I felt a rush of excitement as I opened the door slightly and asked,

"What's the password?"

Carl's voice was deep, resonant and rather sexy, as he said,

"By the pricking of my thumbs, something wicked this way comes."

I pulled the mask down over my eyes, and opened the door fully. I heard him enter the room, then close and lock the door. Cautiously, I walked in the direction of the bed and when I felt its edge, carefully climbed onto it.

Carl guided me on the bed, and arranged the pillows so that when I lay back I was not flat but raised up as if I were about to watch television. He held my left wrist, and I heard the metallic, seductive snap of handcuffs as he cuffed me to the bedpost and did the same with my right wrist. The cool metal rubbed my skin, and the handcuffs jangled when I moved my arms. I could hear the rustle of clothes, indicating Carl was undressing.

The bed dipped – he sat alongside me. The ribbon at my neck was untied, and my negligee fell open, exposing my body. I felt vulnerable knowing he was looking at me, at the way he had bound me to the bed and how I was there for him to do as he wished. It was incredibly exciting, not knowing when he was going to touch me or where and whether he would enter me with his tongue, fingers or cock.

I felt his breath on me, then his large hands groped my breasts, squeezing the flesh and pulling at my nipples. Then I felt his teeth gently, but painfully, bite my erect nipples and hair brushed against my breasts. Carl had a beard, I thought, as he scratched my skin with its bristles. The roughness made me purr with delight. He caressed, sucked, tweaked and pinched until I was moaning and tried to wriggle my inflamed nipples from his grasp. The handcuffs jangled as I writhed.

Carl straddled me, his knees pressed against my sides. As one hand fondled my breasts, I felt his other slide down between my thighs. The anticipation was thrilling. I parted my legs even further, ready for his fingers. When he touched me, I jolted up with desire. His fingers explored my pussy circling my clit and crept closer to my opening. I was already panting with lust, but when he plunged his fingers deep inside me, I gasped loudly, my mouth wide with longing. He withdrew his fingers and paused; I was desperate and when he finally ploughed them back inside me, again, I let out a loud moan of pleasure. He finger-fucked me, just enough to make me wonderfully wet and make me whimper beneath him. When he withdrew his fingers, I waited impatiently for them to open me up and explore my pussy again. He shoved them back deep inside, and I shuddered once more. As I let out a cry of passion at the glorious sensations between my legs, he forced the tip of his erect cock into my mouth.

I took him greedily into my mouth. His hand left my throbbing pussy, to steady himself against the wall. I closed my lips around his thick member, delighted to discover his massive size. He fucked my mouth, withdrawing slowly and then pushing himself in. His cock slid over my tongue, and edged its way to the back of my throat. I swirled my tongue around the sensitive tip of his large cock head and listened to him moan. I imagined what I looked like: sitting up naked in bed, blindfolded, my wrists handcuffed to the bed, Carl straddling me with his hard cock deep in my mouth. The image excited me, and I sucked him even harder.

"Yes," he moaned. "This is what your mouth is for. It wants to be fucked." He pushed harder and faster as I sucked, licked and teased, wanting all of his enormous cock in my mouth. His breathing was ragged, and he moaned louder. I could tell from his frantic thrusting that he was ready and, almost at once, I felt him shudder in my mouth and his thick come pump down my throat.

"You are so sexy Caroline," he murmured. "I've been thinking about this for so long, what I was going to do to you once I'd handcuffed you to the bed."

He squeezed my breasts roughly, and I felt how turned on he was from this scenario; me willingly offering myself to him. We had exchanged numerous emails over the previous weeks so that I felt I knew Carl really well; knew so much about him apart from what he looked like. And, now, I was beginning to know about what he liked to do in the bedroom.

His hands caressed the flesh between my thighs, and creeped up tantalizingly towards my eager pussy. I moaned with delight as he started to massage it, caressing my lips and slipping his fingers in. He worked me well, made me pant and gasp as I writhed and twisted on the bed. The sound of the metal handcuffs were loud in the room as I strained with desire. I wished I could see him; to be able to look at his face and into his eyes as he took my arousal to its peak. He lifted my legs, placed them on his shoulders and I felt his huge cock nudge against me. He teased me, rubbing himself against my opening, against my clit, making me wait. Then as I groaned with pleasure and bit my lip, he pushed himself in deep, right up to the hilt, stretching and filling me.

"This is what your pussy is for; this is what your pussy wants. It wants to be fucked."

Carl fucked me, hard and fast. Ramming into me, he banged my pussy relentlessly. I loved it, crying out my encouragement as he slammed his big, solid cock into my hot, tight hole. Hard thrust after hard thrust, over and over, his full length elicited wave after wave of lustful pleasure. He slowed down and I realized he was close to coming but didn't wish to yet. When he was composed, he fucked me again, still hard. He pounding me ruthlessly, panting and groaning noisily until he was about to come and then he slowed down, only to thrust viciously moments later.

Being bound and blindfolded, having to take what Carl gave me, took me to the edge and when he rubbed his finger on my clit I screamed, my orgasm immediate and intense. My body arched, and I felt the metal of the handcuffs digging into my wrists. I writhed and jerked, my pussy muscles involuntarily clutching at his cock and he brutally fucked me through my climax as he came deep inside me.

He collapsed on top of me, his breathing heavy and labored, when the alarm on my phone rang out. Carl removed the handcuffs from my wrists, and I eagerly pulled off my mask. He stood by the bed: a dark-haired, good-looking man in his early thirties. With his beard and engaging smile, he reminded me of

Jake Gyllenhaal. I was mightily impressed with what I saw, and incredibly impressed with what he had done to me. Unabashed, I stared at his huge, glistening erect cock that had recently ravished my mouth and my pussy. I wanted more – surely, Carl was my perfect lover. Sam would have to be amazing to beat this man.

***

Three knocks at the door – I rushed over and asked for the password.

"*Oh what a tangled web we weave, when first we practice to deceive.*"

Sam had an Irish lilt when he spoke, a mellifluous sing-song voice. I pulled down the mask over my eyes and opened the door. Hesitantly, I made my way to the bed aware that he stood behind me. I lay back on the bed, and waited nervously. My negligee was untied and pulled away from my breasts so that I lay naked and on view.

I shivered with delight, as something light and silky was trailed up my legs, over my stomach and across my breasts. I guessed Sam had brought a silk scarf with him for bondage. He gently tickled it over my body, and I was surprised at the lightness of touch and how sensuous I found it. Then Sam lifted my legs up and bent them so that my knees were adjacent to my breasts. He moved my arms so that I hugged my legs in place. The scarf was tied around one wrist, over the headboard and then around my other wrist. I was secured to the bed with my bottom slightly raised and my pussy on display, unable to lower my legs or move my arms. He had positioned me so that I held my legs spread for him with my sex pouting open. Giving him easy access excited me immensely. I was sure I would be wet before he even touched me.

"Aaahh!" I cried out. Sam had poured icy cold liquid over my breasts and mouth. I licked my lips and swallowed. It was wine. He drizzled some more over my mouth, and this time when I licked my lips, my tongue met his. I opened my mouth waiting for a kiss, but received only wine. He teased me, his tongue darting across my lips, but whenever I opened my mouth he withdrew.

"Tease," I complained. The next time he flicked my lips with his tongue, I moaned. Sam pressed ice cubes to my nipples, making them stiffen. He twirled the cubes repeatedly over them, until they were completely erect. Sam poured more wine over my breasts and licked it away, his tongue making large circles that became smaller until he finished at my nipples, which he sucked. Gently, he massaged my breasts, his fingers barely touched my skin, just lightly brushing my nipples until they ached and burned with desire.

The icy cold wine hitting my hot pussy made me jump. Sam massaged me, and trickled more wine over my pussy. It was bliss when his tongue lapped at the wine, teasing and tickling my flesh. Unlike Carl, Sam was clean shaven and the softness of his skin rubbed against my inner thighs. He kissed, licked and nibbled, then rotated his tongue around my throbbing clit as I panted and gasped with pleasure. He penetrated my pussy with his fingers, easing them slowly in and out of my pussy, before picking up to a frenetic finger fucking of my wet vulva. The licking and fingering made me moan, rapidly taking me to the cusp of an orgasm but before I started to climax, Sam slowed down and the feeling subsided.

Sam discovered quickly from my moans and twitching body how to kiss and finger my pussy to get me to the edge. He sensed when I was dangerously close and would stop at the last moment, leaving me on the brink. It was as if he were playing a game, seeing how long he could keep me going without tipping me over the edge. I became desperate with desire. My pussy ached, wanting to be filled and stretched. I regretted being tied up because I wanted to grab him, pull him on top of me, wrap my legs around his waist and dig my nails into his shoulders as he fucked me hard. As he took me to the cusp again, throatily I pleaded,

"Fuck me, please fuck me."

Instead, Sam released me, letting my imminent orgasm abate again. When he knew I was ready, he slid his fingers inside me again, but this time arched them towards the front of my pussy wall. I cried out, as instantly he hit my G-spot. Relentlessly, he pressed against it, his fingers made a rolling action and I felt an almost painful sensation as he worked me into a frenzy. I cried out. It was wonderful but also uncomfortable; I was so close to a climax but unable to trigger it. I swore as I tried unsuccessfully to gain relief from his stimulation.

"I need to come. I need to come," I whimpered finally.

Sam continued to play with my G-spot but now, at the same time, slid the forefinger of his other hand between my buttocks and deep into my puckered hole. Immediately, it heightened the feeling within my sex, and urged on by my frantic cries, he mercilessly teased my G-spot and finger-fucked my ass.

I wanted to see; I wanted to see how I looked, trussed up like a turkey with my pussy and ass on display while Sam penetrated me with his fingers and made me scream. It was the perfect position. He did as he pleased – and I could do nothing, nothing but submit to his playful will. I pulled against my restraints as the rising sensation flooded my body. Sam bit my nipples, but the pleasure outweighed the pain. How much more could I take? It was too good, too unbearably good.

Sam licked my fleshy labia, and nibbled my clit as he continued to press my sweet spot and explored the depths of my ass with his probing forefinger. I came at once; an intense orgasm that made me scream and try to break free, but I was bound tightly to the bed. He continued to lick and finger me, keeping his mouth firmly clamped to my pussy. Sam kept me coming, for much longer than I could bear.

"No, no, stop, stop," I begged.

He withdrew his fingers from my ass, and my aching, sopping wet pussy. My heart hammered and I breathed deeply, calming down when, suddenly, he slid his fingers back into my pussy and tapped my G-spot. I writhed as the aftershock rocked my body. He withdrew his fingers, and I relaxed. Sam licked my clit vigorously to force the next aftershock, I moaned and shook. He let me relax, before he slid his finger into my tight ass while stroking my sensitive and swollen pussy.

"Oh God," I groaned. "It's too much."

But he continued, forcing aftershock followed by

aftershock. Sam let me recover for several seconds then shoved another finger deep within my holes, or licked me lustily, or tweaked my nipples, or smacked my pussy or poured wine over my clit. Something unexpected so that I writhed and moaned more.

I was exhausted, unable to believe he had done that to me with only his fingers and tongue.

The alarm on my phone startled me. Sam removed my eye mask, and stood by the bed but made no attempt to untie me. I smiled widely as I looked at the small boyish frame, angular hips, smooth translucent skin and piercing blue eyes.

"Hello!" I said with surprise. "I'm guessing Sam is short for Samantha and not Samuel?"

"Yeah," she said, sitting on the bed. Sam wore black boots, jeans and a white vest that emphasized her small, pert breasts. I hadn't realized that she hadn't undressed. She was petite and pretty with short, glossy black hair.

"But I definitely heard a man at the door," I commented. "A man with an Irish accent."

She reached for her backpack, and from it withdrew a digital voice recorder. She pressed a button and I heard a man say,

"Oh what a tangled web we weave, when first we practice to deceive."

"My colleague Cormac," she shrugged. "I asked him to record the message."

"Oh!" I said still struggling to comprehend the situation. "Are you going to untie me now?"

"No," she replied. "Would you like some wine? I'm going to have some."

I looked down at my naked, bound body. My

bared pussy still on display, I felt slightly embarrassed which was ridiculous as Sam – female Sam – had just played with it undisturbed for an hour.

Turning my head, I saw that she had the wine bottle in her hand. She tipped it, and wine sloshed over my breasts. Without a word she bent over and licked them dry, I felt the pricking, aching desire begin to form. She rolled my nipples between her forefingers and thumbs and, involuntarily, I let slip a moan of pleasure.

"I wrote to you because I really liked your internet profile," she said. "We had an immediate online rapport. We got on really well. I knew I really wanted to meet you." She pulled off her vest, and I admired her breasts, wanted to suck them and tease them in the same way that she had teased mine with her fingers.

Sam watched me squirm with delight as she rolled them vigorously and continued, "When you wrote to say that you would be in a hotel, blindfolded and that I could tie you up and do whatever I wanted to you, I knew it was the ideal opportunity. I could show you that I would be your perfect lover. I could give you everything you wanted."

She stood up and removed her boots and jeans. Looking at her naked body, I started to feel the tingle of arousal deep within my pussy.

"You enjoyed what I just did to you." Sam slid her fingers between my labia and felt my wetness, and laughed. "And you want more!"

I nodded.

"Yes, I loved it. It was unbelievable." I looked earnestly into her eyes. "And I want more," I confessed.

She threw the eye mask on to the floor.

"I'm not going to put the blindfold back on, because I want you to watch me. I want you to see exactly what I'm doing to you. Do you want me to reset the timer on your phone?"

"Oh no," I smiled. "You can take as long as you like."

She delved into her backpack, pulling out a harness, which she strapped around her waist. Attached to the front was a large, black dildo. My heart raced when I saw it.

"Earlier you begged me to fuck you, and now I'm going to," she stated simply.

I watched silently as she climbed on to the bed.

"You like this, don't you?" Sam said as she plunged her fingers in and out of my pussy. "And you certainly love this." She drummed on my G-spot. Within seconds I writhed, desperate for more. Sam continued playing with me, teasing and tormenting me, taking me to the brink and holding me there until, finally, I shouted,

"This is what my pussy is for; this is what my pussy wants. It wants to be fucked."

She moved to the foot of the bed, positioning the dildo at my opening.

"I think it's only fair that later on I tie you to the bed and do whatever I want to you." I breathed deeply.

Sam smiled broadly.

"Only when you've knocked three times and said the password."

And, with that comment my perfect lover slowly eased into my hungry, wet pussy.

Cops and Robbers
By Oleander Plume

A breeze blew in from the open window and brushed across my naked cock, giving me a slight boner. I suppose you could call that a testament to how horny I was, since all it took to get me going was a slight movement of air. I knew sleep would be impossible until I had a good wank, so I spit on my fingers and went to work. I was five minutes in, hot, sweaty and ready to burst, when a strange noise from outside made my hips freeze and my cop instincts kick into overdrive. I did a ninja roll off the bed, crept to the window and peered outside. From my vantage point on the second floor, I could see a shadowy figure cutting across my neighbor's backyard, heading for the patio door.

I fumbled around in the dark until I found my uniform pants in a tangled wad next to my bed. Somehow I managed to yank them on while heading downstairs, pausing along the way to stuff my half erect cock inside and zip up. Adrenaline pumping, I hopped the fence in time to see the perp's feet disappear through an open window. I waited a few minutes, then slithered in after him. Through the dim light, I saw that he was tall, roughly six foot, with a slim build and broad shoulders. Without taking my eyes off him, I reached for my gun, but came up empty. The image of my piece resting in my nightstand drawer, made me perform a mental head slap. Since I wasn't armed, I did the only thing I could do, tackled him from behind.

"What the fuck are you doing?"

He had the kind of voice that made my balls ache.

"Me? I caught you breaking and entering." He struggled like mad while my sweaty hands fumbled with the cuffs that were hanging from my belt loop. A loud meow broke my concentration, and I was startled when something furry rubbed against my bare feet. "What the fuck is that?"

"That's Mr. Jingles. I'm here to feed him while Rick and Cindy are on their honeymoon, but I forgot my key."

"Sure, I believe you, pal." The cat mewled louder, sounding more like a grizzly bear than a feline. "Pfffft, Mr. Jingles."

"Hey, I didn't give him that stupid name."

While I struggled with the would-be perp, Mr. Jingles roared and nudged me with his rather bulbous body.

"He's hungry. At least let me up so I can feed him." I freed the cuffs and managed to clamp one bracelet on his left wrist. Mr. Jingles whined mournfully. "Don't you hear him crying?"

I glanced at the cat, who was about the size of a Volkswagen. "That fat son of a bitch? I don't think starving is in his imminent future."

I sat on the perp's thighs, and shackled his wrists behind his back. Even in the dim light, I could tell he was muscular, and got a little turned on from the feel of his hard body under my legs. Okay, a lot turned on, even from the back, the dude was hot. The fact that only a few layers of fabric separated my cock from his ass didn't help, either.

"What's your name?"

"Sean Flannity. Could you please get off me? You're crushing my legs."

I stood up, helping him to his feet.

"Now what?"

"Now, I call a squad car."

"But, I swear, I'm here to feed the cat." Mr. Jingles wove in and out between Sean's legs. "See? He knows me."

"Yeah, sure he does."

I dragged him into the kitchen, and fumbled for the light switch. When I finally got a decent look at him, I almost swooned like a teenaged girl. Not only was he hot, he was smokin' hot with glossy brown hair streaked with blonde, bright blue eyes and a tat peeking out from one sleeve. I wondered if he had ink anywhere else and what it would taste like under my tongue. I'm a sucker for tattoos. And bad boys. My balls throbbed, and I almost forgot why I was there, until the damn cat started wailing like a furry banshee. Sean nodded toward the kitchen counter, where a giant stack of tin cans was waiting, along with a note.

Sean, please feed Mr. Jingles only once a day, he's on a diet. Don't forget to change his water. Thanks again, Cindy and Rick.

I pinched the bridge of my nose and groaned.

"Shit. Do you have any ID on you?"

"No, I forgot my wallet and Rick's key. I live in

one of the new apartments on Willow, and since it was a nice night, I decided to walk here. Luckily, the window was open."

I hated to admit it, but the guy looked honest and the cat did seem to like him. A lot. I unlocked the cuffs and turned him loose.

"Do you always rough up innocent citizens like that?"

He rubbed his wrists and pouted at me.

"Sorry, but I'm a cop and I saw you climb through a window. What would you have done?"

"I guess I would have done the same. Rick will be glad to hear you're looking out for him."

"Which is why I'm going to stick around until you're finished, just to be sure."

He shot me a sexy smile. "Go ahead, I don't mind." His eyes traveled down to my bare chest, then lower. "I don't mind at all."

"I sense we play for the same team." I smiled back at him.

He licked his lips as he ran his index finger down my sternum.

"I'd like to play, but I should feed Mr. Jingles first."

He filled the cat's dish with a gray blob that smelled like a dumpster, then washed and refilled the water bowl. Mr. Jingles buried his face into the pile of mystery meat, and purred like a buzz saw.

"Well, the cat's happy."

Sean rested both of his wrists on my shoulders.

"I'd like to make you happy now."

"Sounds good to me."

"What's your name, handsome?"

"Luis."

"Luis," he repeated.

"I like the way my name sounds coming out of your mouth."

He closed his eyes when he leaned in to kiss me. Fuck his lips were hot! I deepened the kiss, and explored his pouty bottom lip with my tongue. He moved in closer until his firm bulge was bumping up against mine.

"Luis, I want to fuck you, right in this kitchen."

"Maybe I want to fuck you first."

"Sorry, I already called dibs. You do bottom, right?" The way he tilted his head at me was adorable, and I swooned again.

"Sure, sometimes." I didn't want to admit how much I love getting my ass fucked, I'm sort of a slut that way. Sure, I like to plug a guy's hole once in a while, but I prefer to catch, if you know what I mean. "I don't have a condom."

"I'm sure Rick has some upstairs in his bedroom. Let's go and find out."

"This isn't cool, I shouldn't be doing this," I said while we pawed through all the dresser drawers. The one on the bottom right turned out to be a treasure trove of kink. "Whoa."

"We found somebody's naughty drawer," Sean said in a singsong voice. He picked up a large vibrator and waved it at me. "Who do you think uses this?"

"That's the Ram-Master 2000, I have one of those at home."

"You do?" Sean giggled.

"I have a naughty drawer, too. Maybe I'll let you rifle through it sometime."

Sean dangled a pair of pink, furry handcuffs in front of my face. "I'd love to see you in these."

I held up my regulation cuffs.

"Pink isn't my color, but you can use these, kinky boy." My dick turned to cement, overjoyed at the thought of a little tie-up fun.

"Get naked, and I'll cuff you to the bed." I dropped my pants and he whistled. "Wow, Luis, you have a nice sized cock."

"Show me yours."

He did have more tattoos besides the one on his arm; a sun circled his belly button, and a rope of barbed wire circled one muscular thigh. He looked about as delicious as a hot fudge sundae, and the cherry on top was his cock, a masterpiece of skin and throbbing veins that kept growing. Once that fucker was fully erect, I backpedaled.

"Holy sweet shit on a cracker, I think I've changed my mind. I'll top you."

Sean ran his fingers over his dick.

"Too much meat for you? I'll go slow and use lots of lube. There's plenty, see?"

He held up a gigantic bottle of clear liquid.

"Wow, I had no idea Rick and Cindy were into stuff that required so much lube!"

"Oh, Cindy's a real slut." Sean pulled me close for another hot kiss, then pushed me onto the bed. "Let's get you restrained."

"Yeah, baby, then you can have your way with me."

He looped the handcuffs through a railing on the wrought iron headboard, and attached them to my wrists.

"Comfy?"

"Very."

"Good." He grinned and patted my cheek. "Boy, you are the biggest dumb ass I've ever met."

"Say what?"

"I've been casing this neighborhood for over a month." He laughed while he put his clothes back on. "Rick puts everything on Facebook, and I do mean everything."

"Fuck!" I felt like such an idiot. To further the indignity of the situation, Mr. Jingles jumped on the bed and rubbed himself against my bare thigh. "So, you're a professional thief? Figures."

"And you're not a very good cop!"

I watched while he rummaged through the closet. Damn, he had a nice ass. I struggled, then remembered that I'd let him use my own fucking handcuffs. He was right, I was a big dumb ass.

"Fucking bastard, let me go!"

He paused and took a long look at my dick.

"I would be a cruel bastard if I left you with blue balls, maybe I should take care of you first."

"Stay the fuck away from me," was what I said out loud. Mentally, I was begging for him to fuck me into the next century.

"Are you sure?" He unzipped and pulled out his giant meat stick. I tried not to drool while he stroked it back into hardness. "You want this, don't you?"

"Do I have a choice?"

He smiled and shook his head.

"None whatsoever."

"Bring it, bitch."

He took his time rolling on a condom and lubing up, the wait would have been torture, but I was too busy admiring his delicious dick to notice. Damn, that thing was fat with a shaved scrotum so swollen it appeared bruised. The thought of it slapping against my ass made me put my legs up in the air, giving him an open invitation to enter.

"Aren't you the little slut?"

"Shut up and fuck me already."

He stared into my eyes while he pushed the head of his cock against my opening. As much as I wanted him inside, the girth of his cockhead made me clench. I bit my lip and whimpered.

"You're not ready, let me fix that." He poured lube on his fingers, and began massaging my asshole. "Relax, let me stretch you."

I squeezed my eyes shut when his fingers slid inside, enjoying and hating the burning pressure. Mr. Jingles curled up next to my head and meowed in my ear. He smelled like dead fish.

"Get away from me, cat."

"I can't blame him for wanting to watch. I've never seen a cop as hot as you, well, maybe in a porno, but certainly not in real life."

His fingers went deeper and he rubbed my chest with his other hand, pinching my nipples with just enough force to make me tingle all over. I loved being restrained with his mouth clamped on mine, and his fingers invading my hungry ass. I felt like he owned me, and I loved it.

"How hard do you want me to make you come?"

"Just fuck me." My voice was more of a whine, which surprised me. I had never begged. Until Sean. He made me beg like a starving dog.

"You want my big hard cock up your tight little ass?"

"Uh huh." More whining, fuck, I wanted him so bad.

"You want me to fuck you nice and deep until you shoot your load all over your hot body?"

He kissed my nipples, while he peered up at me. All I could do was nod.

"I want that too, Luis. I want to make you scream out my name."

"I don't even know your name."

"It's actually Sean, kind of a coincidence, huh?" He glossed his dick with more lube, I pulled my legs back and opened myself for him.

"Don't make me wait any more."

His cockhead pushed at my hole, and I was ready. I closed my eyes and focused on the sensation of it spreading me open, filling me to capacity as it slid in deep. My back arched and my nipples hardened into tight points, I think my toes even curled.

"Fuck, you feel good, so tight."

He pulled me up by my shoulders, and kissed me again. Our tongues fought against each other for position. His won, slipping inside my mouth like a small fist. I groaned, and felt my balls tighten.

"I'm gonna come."

"No, not yet." He pulled out, leaving just his tip inside my throbbing anus. "Look at me."

I opened my eyes and stared into his. They were dark blue, fringed with impossibly long lashes. He had freckles scattered across the bridge of his nose, and a small scar under his left eye that I couldn't help but kiss. I heard his breath catch in his chest as I whispered against his skin.

"You're beautiful, Sean. Why did you have to be a thief?"

"Why did you have to be a cop?"

He drove back in, then out, over and over until I almost screamed. His movements were slow and silky, teasing me into madness. Finally, he drove balls deep, and gave me the pummeling I was desperately craving. He didn't just hit my sweet spot, he crushed it, sending me into the hardest orgasm I ever had in my life. He milked so much semen out of me, I half expected to crumble into dust.

"Holy hell, Sean that was so good." He pulled out and yanked the rubber off his rock hard dick. "Put it in my mouth."

He straddled my face and I inhaled his cock, but I couldn't deep throat it. I gagged a little.

"Just suck the tip, I'm so fucking close."

A few draws with my mouth, and his semen filled my mouth. His soft, breathy moans caused a weird sensation in my chest area, almost as if I was falling for him. As I swallowed his load, he stroked my hair and whispered my name,

"Luis, your mouth is as sweet as your ass."

He lifted his cock out of the way, and rested his scrotum against my lips. I gladly licked it all over. "Fuck, that's good, my balls are still twitching."

"How about taking off these cuffs, and we'll both go home, no harm, no foul."

"I can't, Luis. My rent is due and my fridge is empty. There are enough electronic goodies in this place to keep a roof over my head for the next two months. Sorry, babe, but it sure was fun."

He kissed me, and I growled at him.

"You can't leave me here like this, you fucking prick!"

"You're right."

He wiped the jizz off my chest with a wad of toilet paper, and covered me up with the bedspread. "I'll call 911 after I leave. I'm sure your cop friends will be talking about this for a long, long time."

"You'd better watch your back, asshole, because one day you're gonna find my gun stuck in it."

He kissed me again, a lover's kiss filled with sweetness that I didn't expect. My ass was raw after being so righteously fucked.

But I wanted more.

When he walked out, my heart ached even more than my balls. While I laid there, fuming, I could hear him downstairs ransacking the place. Mr. Jingles curled up on my chest and purred.

"Hey, fat bastard, unlock these cuffs, will ya?" He just blinked his yellow eyes at me. "Fuck."

I tried to come up with a plausible excuse for being handcuffed and naked in my neighbor's bed, but came up short. My eyes grew heavy, and between the warmth of the blanket, the afterglow and the hypnotic droning of Mr. Jingles, I drifted off.

I woke up at 4:00 a.m., with one hand free, and the other cuffed to the headboard. The stupid cat was sprawled across my ankles, and there was a note on the pillow next to me.

Luis:

I decided to cut you a break. You're welcome.

- Sean

PS: You're adorable when you're sleeping. I took pictures!

"Mother fucker!" I found the key to the cuffs under the note. Mr. Jingles howled in protest when I moved. "Shut up, you fat bastard."

After freeing myself and yanking on pants, I did a quick run through of the house, but couldn't find anything missing. The plasma screen still hung on the wall in the living room, the jewelry box appeared intact and an expensive camera was sitting untouched on a desk in the home office. No evidence, no crime, which made my life a lot easier. I didn't feel guilty about keeping it to myself.

I went home and slept until 10:00 a.m., dreaming about Sean. When I woke up, I still couldn't drive him out of my head. The spent feeling in my asshole didn't help. either. It had been such a satisfying fuck, I wanted him again.

Two days later, a loud thud woke me up. I grabbed my cuffs, and crept out into the hallway. Someone was in my house. My heart raced as I stealthily tread down the stairs, then almost beat out of my chest when I glimpsed the dark figure in my living room. I bolted forward, and knocked him down in a football tackle. He barely struggled when I cuffed his hands behind his back.

"Oh, darn, you caught me!" said the familiar sexy voice.

"Sean? Are you fucking nuts? Why would you break into a cop's house?"

I rolled him onto his back, and he grinned at me.

"Gonna turn me in?" Once again, the feeling of him under me got my motor running.

"For what? You didn't steal anything, at least, not that I could tell."

"You're right."

He licked his lips as he stared at me.

"What the fuck kind of game are you playing?"

"Look, I had every intention of robbing the place... I'm not sure why I didn't."

"I'm gonna have to, uh, I mean I should really—"

Staring into those blue eyes of his rendered me stupid. He rolled his eyes and sighed,

"Just kiss me."

I did. I kissed him sloppily with lots of tongue, as we rolled around on the floor making out.

"I should turn you in."

I kissed his chin.

"Fuck me first."

"Then I'll never want to turn you in."

I licked along his jawline.

"Make up your mind, I'm horny as hell."

"Technically there was no crime. Right?"

I nibbled his bottom lip while I squeezed his ass.

"Right. I didn't steal anything."

"Why? And tell me the truth this time."

"I figured if I was going to have a cop for a boyfriend, I should clean up my act."

I froze, and a warmth I hadn't felt in a long time spread out all over my body.

"Oh, baby, let me take these cuffs off you, and these clothes."

"The clothes can go, leave the cuffs on, it's so fucking sexy." His shoes, socks, jeans, and underwear were easy to take off. His tee shirt was another story. "Tear it off me, Luis."

I ripped it down the center, exposing his muscular chest. I spent the next several minutes rubbing his pecs, and chewing on his nipples.

"Fuck me."

The desperate tone in his voice was like mine begging him the first night we met. I decided to torture him for a while, just for fun. I kissed my way down to his dick.

"Not yet. I need to taste you again."

I buried my tongue in his dripping slit, he tasted like a saline lollipop. My mouth explored every inch, from the tip of his shaft to his velvety taint. Then lower. He raised his legs to give me better access to his asshole, I stuffed my tongue inside and he groaned.

"I'm gonna rim you until you come all over."

"No." His eyes were wild, his face flushed. "I want to come when you're fucking me. I'm so close, please, take me hard, right here on the floor."

I chuckled while I licked harder.

"I'm calling the shots this time." I teased his pink opening with my fingertip. "It's so pretty, baby, let me give it some attention."

The sexy noises he made while I licked and sucked his ass drove me crazy. Soft breathy moans, high-pitched sighs mingled with low growls. Occasionally he would whisper my name, which caused a flutter in my heart and my testicles. Finally, I couldn't take it anymore.

"Are you ready for me to fuck your ass?"

I gave him a small spank on one round ass cheek.

"Fuck, yeah."

I sprinted upstairs, grabbed a condom and lube. When I returned to him, he was face down on the floor, tan legs spread wide, white ass gyrating below his bound wrists. The vision of him fucking the carpet almost caused me to shoot my load.

"Holy shit, those are some sexy tan lines, baby."

He lifted his head and smiled.

"Hurry up and fuck me."

"You sure this is how you want it? The bed is much more comfortable."

"This is perfect, I want to feel you on top of me while you fuck me hard."

"Okay, okay. Give me a sec." I rolled on a condom and lubed up, then poured some down his crack and rubbed it into his hole. "Let me get you ready."

"I'm ready now."

His whine was sexy enough to cause my dick to jump. I lay next to him, and massaged his ass while I kissed his shoulder.

He turned his head and looked at me.

"Why are you so sexy?"

"I'm Spanish, we're all this way." I slipped a finger inside him, he panted softly and ground his cock into the rug. "Sweet baby, you're so horny."

"Kiss me." He wagged his tongue at me.

I stretched out next to him, and fingered his asshole while I sucked his tongue. He kept grinding away on the carpet.

"I'm getting jealous of the rug!"

"Fuck me, then, I need to come. Are you going to make me come?"

I straddled his thighs and planted my hands on the floor.

"I'm going to make you come, baby, so hard, are you ready for me?"

I moved my hips back and forth, teasing his ass crack with my cock.

"Don't piss me off, fuck me!"

I held myself up with one hand, and used the other to guide my cock inside his hole. Once I had the tip in position, I slid in deep, then stayed still to give him a chance to adjust.

"You feel so good, Sean."

"Mmm, Luis, it's so big and hard. Put all your weight on me, I want it."

I did what he asked, but his fingers dug into my stomach, so I leaned up again and thrust in short, gentle strokes.

"Harder, Luis." I quickened my pace. "Yeah, like that, just like that."

I felt like I was like fucking velvet. He clamped around me, squeezing my full length with perfect force. I bent my elbows to kiss his neck while I pumped. He chanted under his breath in rhythm with my fucking,

"Fuck, fuck, fuck, fuck, fuck." Low and breathy, as if each thrust of my dick pushed the word from his throat. "Fuck, fuck, fuck, fuck, fuck."

I paused.

"Am I hurting you?"

"No, so good, more, don't stop, don't you fucking stop!"

I ground against him, pushing him into the floor. I wondered if his imprint would linger in the carpet forever, I was fucking him with such force. His chant changed as he headed closer to orgasm,

"Yeah, yeah, yeah, yeah, yeah." He repeated endlessly, like a sexy metronome. "Yeah, yeah, yeah, yeah, fuck yeah."

"Keep talking like that baby, you're driving me

crazy." I matched his tempo. "Are you going to come for me?" His head lifted as his back arched.

"Yeah. Uhn, oh fuck, Luis, it's so good!"

I licked the tan skin on his shoulder, he tasted like heat, sunlight and every delicious thing that existed in the world. I wanted to bite into his skin and eat him alive. Instead, I nibbled on the back of his neck, while he writhed under me.

"Luis!"

His tight hole clenched, and he growled like an animal.

"What, baby?"

"I'm coming!"

The words came out in a breathless rush.

"Do it, Sean, come for me." He buried his face in the rug, and shrieked my name as he came. "There, baby, that's it."

He clamped down on me so tight, it caused a familiar itch deep in my balls and I knew I was falling over the edge. I squeezed my eyes shut, holding my breath as I fell into bliss.

"Fuck!"

I came so hard I thought my balls were turning inside out. I dug my fingers into the carpet, and clenched my teeth while the last bits shot out.

"Luis," Sean whimpered. "Oh, my god, Luis."

"I'm going to get the key, I'll be right back."

"No, leave them on for a little longer." He rolled onto his side. "Hold me."

I wrapped my arms around him, then flipped over, putting his trembling body on top of mine.

"Are you okay?"

"That was the best fuck I've ever had, though I

trashed your rug!" He giggled as he nuzzled my chin.

"It was?"

"Fuck yeah, your dick fit inside me so perfectly. You worked over my sweet spot so much, I came twice. Twice! That's never happened to me before."

"You're a fucking sex machine, Sean. Damn." I stroked his hair and his back he was so silky everywhere, I felt as I massaged his arms. "Let me unlock these."

"I'm ready now, my shoulders are cramping."

Later that night, we were snuggled up in my bed, naked skin touching, soft kisses and gentle touches. I could feel myself falling for him. Hard. But I was a cop, and he was a criminal.

"Sean, if you need money, I can help you out. You don't need to rob people."

"Yeah, about that, I lied." He kissed my chest. "Just a little. Don't be mad."

More kisses. I couldn't have been mad if I tried.

"Which part did you lie about?"

"I'm not a thief. Rick and Cindy are my friends. I've seen you before. Hell, I beat off in Rick's bathroom while I watched you mow your lawn. He mentioned you were gay, and I said I was interested. Cindy was planning on fixing us up once they got back from the Bahamas."

"So you weren't breaking in?"

"No, I really did forget my key, that part was all true. But, seeing you handcuffed, well, that's when the whole naughty idea popped in my head."

I smiled, and I couldn't stop.

"So why did you run off?"

"I didn't. I went downstairs and banged around a

bit, just to make it look good. When I came back upstairs, you were sound asleep. I tried everything to wake you up, but you were comatose."

I was stunned, in a good way. Thrilled was probably a better word. He wasn't a criminal, and he liked me. I tickled his ribs, and he giggled.

"Naughty boy, you really had me fooled!"

"Rick has a key to your place, that's how I got in here tonight. I was going to sneak into your bed, but I bashed my shin on your coffee table."

"You scared the crap out of me!"

"Next thing I know, you were on top of me. Which is exactly what I was hoping for!"

I kissed every inch of his face. "You could have just knocked on my door, you know."

"Wasn't my way a lot more fun?"

"Yes, it was."

I pinned him under me, and stared into his blue eyes. That's when I fell, so hard I thought my bones would shatter as I made impact.

"When I wake up in the morning, will you still be here?"

"Yes, of course. You're stuck with me now."

I waited until he fell asleep, then cuffed him to the headboard.

Just to be sure.

Coming Down Fast

By Kaysee Renee Robichaud

Roy tugged on one of the straps encircling Sally's shoulders, cinching it tighter than she had, and the effect was the same as pulling on a pet leash: an undeniable attention grabber. "Pop quiz," he said for the third time since takeoff. In lieu of an actual question, he indicated one of the lines on his chest, while the airplane's engines whirred and droned in the Jeopardy theme (the mile high techno-mechanical remix, Sally considered it after receiving so many pop quizzes).

The line in question terminated in a red and white handle, solid looking but not cumbersome. Anchor shaped for easy gripping and tugging. Impossible to ignore when needed. Sally pursed her lips. "The reserve chute line?"

"Outstanding," he replied. He was a good-looking man with brown eyes that could be gentle or stern as the situation demanded. His brush cut emphasized the smallness of his ears and the narrowness of his face. The hairstyle choice was a leftover of what he referred to as his "misspent youth" aboard one of the Navy's floating city aircraft carriers, but a secondary effect from those days was his attention to bodily discipline. He was still in prime fighting trim. He had broad shoulders that could wrestle loose rigging back in place even during high storms, solid arms that could bench two hundred easy, abs and ass tight enough to bounce back tossed change, leg muscles to kill for.

Sally knew she was pretty enough. And not in bad shape, either. She had her sights set on an MMA title, and that demanding exercise regimen weeded out the truly unmotivated. The slick magazines dedicated to her sport enjoyed her bad girl image, casting her as a dark-haired Veronica in a world of Betties, vying for world domination. They played up her height and her build, thankfully playing down the massive ankles she had always hated. Those ankles were a leftover of her father's Scottish heritage, while the rest of her was classic Castilian Spanish beauty with an exotic touch of Syrian.

Headlines of late had been less about her body than the Thrash and Thunder bout this coming weekend, and though she was geeked to be on her way, she was also a bit terrified. The best solution for that? A little special something-something to celebrate six kinky months with the man who really understood her.

His suggestion had surprised her, all right.

"Tell me the routine," he said. Clipped words that were perfect for military leadership or for playing the top role in their bedroom/playroom.

Though the Short SC.7 Skyvan aircraft was a relatively small one, the lack of seats near the rear offered the illusion of space. It was still pretty cozy, and when the airplane heaved a little, she fell right into him. Roy being Roy, he caught her without so much as a grunt.

"You are in control," Sally said.

"Details, please." Though his manner was brusque, he was simply offering her the standard line that all parachuting professionals at Good To The Last Drop gave to their first timers. There were a lot of things to keep straight when performing this sport.

Good To The Last Drop's company literature referred to these as tandem jumps.

"You have control over the main and emergency chutes. I will be tied to you." The rigs were something right off www.ExtremeRestriants.com but made for more than play. Buckles and straps made from solidly designed synthetics and leather. Hers were tight across her torso, with lines that slung around her shoulders and beneath her breasts and between her legs. The world's tightest hug, comforting and compassionate. Just being in her current rig brought her warm squirmies. And soon she would be strapped back-to-belly against her man, and then the two of them would be plummeting through the air together, hoping that the primary or emergency parachute would work. "We go out together, and we arrive together. My life is in your hands. You," she repeated, "are in control."

He flushed with power as she said this again, color burning across his pale cheeks and forehead. He glanced back toward the cockpit, separated from this rear area by a flimsy looking sheet stretched across a curtain rod. Roy had called this "the privacy veil," and explained that it was a mostly ineffective barrier between the crew and the folks, which allowed those mind-changers to "bitch out without 100% embarrassment." Of course, the crew would know when they landed, but there was no real razzing. The shame was born internally. "Cowards die a million times before their deaths," Roy had upped Shakespeare's famous line, "the valiant taste of death only once. And even then, we miss out on the flavor."

"You," she said a third time," are in charge."

Most of her life was spent being the killer queen. In the ring, in the gym, in her 9 to 5 team management gig at the zoo. She had to make decisions, plan out not only her own life but those of people around her. It was a relief to find someone worth giving her trust to.

Like Roy.

"I want you to suck my cock," he said.

"Here?" Her eyes shifted from his to the curtain. Timmy could peek back at any time. "Now?"

"You ever thought about joining the mile high club?" he asked.

When she had been lying in bed with him last Monday, talking about the coming bout and the low level background worries, which had resulted in this surprising skydiving suggestion, she had originally been thinking Roy was asking her to join the ranks of that particular club. Sure, the twin prop they were in was not quite a mile up, but it was close enough for her. However, Roy was firm in his assertions that "Flying at approximately 4000 feet, was nowhere near the 5,280 feet measurement of the according to NIST-OWM mile."

NIST, he had helpfully supplied when her face corkscrewed with confusion at the acronym, stood for the National Institute for Standards and Technology, whose Office of Weights and Measures served as some kind of measurement uniformity authority. She imagined them as a bunch of police officers armed with measuring tapes instead of Tasers, and this made her smile.

The mile high club … did they even have time? They were up here to jump, not get jumped.

Although …

"And who is in control?" His voice was a deep growl. The kind of thing that made her already quivering parts thrum with joy.

In response, she ran her hands down his chest, across his own harness. The bulge below was all Roy, and it was a pleasant treasure to find. Though he was belted in, nothing was close to constricting his junk. That would be a bad idea when the chutes were deployed, he had explained, and the retarding jolt would tug every line to a halt.

His cock was rock hard and ready, and she knelt before him as she freed his shaft. Took that meaty banana's familiar curve between her lips and deep as deep could be. His manhood tasted wonderful, now that they were blood bonded.

She teased him with short strokes and a playful tongue, and he moaned softly for her, trembling and shivering when she wanted him to. Oral sex was not a duty, it was a pleasure. The way Roy got off on her efforts got her off, too. Her body responded to him, sympathy passion.

His hands were firm on her neck and back, playing with her through her clothes. Solid strokes. She took him all the way in, past the point of gag reflex, and a flood of saliva filled her mouth. She held him until the fires caught in her chest, and then she lost control of herself. A little choke pulled him deeper still and a touch of milk spilled down her throat.

Then, he pulled her head off his erection. His strong arms brought her to her feet and into a passionate kiss. While their mouths worked, he teased her back and then her breasts. Using her strap harness rig as he might use a spreader bar to drag her closer, to position her how he wanted.

Then, his fingers worked a little magic, showing her the actual reason he had suggested a certain style of pants. She had been surprised when he provided a pair of olive drab slacks for her. She was usually a fan of more colorful clothing. However, these had a special feature hidden under a cunning elastic patch: the zipper started just below the button and went down and around, stopping just short of the waistline in the rear.

These pants could transform from dressy to open crotch with a simple slip of the zip.

Which was what Roy was doing now.

"Mile high, Sally," he whispered. "Let's take it a mile high."

Her response was a throaty whisper. "Take me, Roy. Take me hard."

His cock was already there, and soon enough, so was the rest of him. He lifted her onto a stack of secured crates. Unzipped and legs spread, he had a nice view of her lacy black panties. Black, of course, because she was feeling naughty today. The lace featured little skulls and roses, a fun mix, but nowhere near as fun as the things his fingers were doing to her. Nudging and teasing and playing along her slit.

She nibbled along his throat, pausing to suck on his Adam's apple, and he replied by tugging her panties aside. Pushing his fingers into her warm, wet place.

Quickies were not usually her preference, but

there was something special about the immediacy here. Something intensely erotic about his riveted attention and the clock ticking in the back of her mind. As well, something thrilling about the thin partition between pilot Timmy and their lust. *Will he even be able to look us straight in the eye after he lands?*

"Fuck me, Roy. Get that dick inside me."

He held her panties aside and teased her slit with his shaft. Rubbing it back and forth, sending tingles straight to her core. Then, he caught hold of her harness and pulled her tight against him. Onto him. Her response was louder than expected, an uncontrollable yelp of pleasured surprise.

Then, he was fucking her. Fast and frantic and perfect. Hotter sex than they had ever had, and the thermometer had broken quite a few times before. The harness was cinched tight around her, the straps confining and comforting. He used them to regulate her speed. When she wanted to go faster, he kept her steady. It drove her wild.

Then, she was coming on him, the smell of their sex flooding the rear compartment.

His hands and his mouth never stopped teasing her. She bit him hard enough to leave round teeth marks. It was amazing.

Suddenly, he was out, and she was turning around, and he finished opening the zipper, baring her ass. His shaft nudged the naughty hole, and she gritted her teeth. This would be rough, maybe even bad rough, but she wanted him. It would hurt like hell later, but damn it all *she wanted him.*

He kept her waiting. The clock ticked off almost twelve seconds in her head before his shaft sank home.

Slid right in without the expected friction burn. Only pleasure.

"Lubed," she squawked, surprised. He had slicked his shaft with some kind of lotion or gel. His firmness filled her ass so nicely. She moaned and shoved back against him, rubbing him. He again caught her by the strap harness rig, using this to control her motions.

"Faster," she pleaded, but he stayed steady.

"Harder," she whispered, but his constancy remained untouched, the denial thrilling her to greater heights still. She came again, keeping the verbal fireworks low and hopefully subtle. Then, he was pulling out of her and pulling her zipper shut before stowing his still engorged cock.

"You ready for the long ride down?" he asked as she straightened her gear.

There was no time for hesitation. No desire to change her mind. Their fucking had touched her somewhere deep, tapping that fear keg and letting the contents drain out. Replacing them, maybe, with something far more hopeful and helpful.

"You are in control."

He snapped clips between their harnesses. This pulled her in still new ways. His erection's bulge was positioned right behind her ass, and she momentarily imagined the two of them fucking all the way down.

Her system as overloaded with stimulation, the straps nice and tight, her warm and wet quim sending out happy vibes. He guided her to the door, checked their straps one more time.

"Remember to keep an eye on your altimeter."

Altimeter? What was that? Oh, yes. The thing on

her arm. A gauge that resembled an analog watch with numbers in the thousands.

"Also remember," he said, "that I have you. You're strapped to me, and I've got you."

They did not seem like the most romantic words she had ever heard before, but right now? With only a slender piece of steel between them and 4000 feet of wind and nothing between them and the ground? They were quite romantic indeed.

She tried to say those three little words, but hesitated too long before starting. She got out the "I" but then the door opened, and the wind screamed before them, and they were jumping out of a plane.

Though Sally had subconsciously expected them to fall straight down, they actually moved parallel to the aircraft as well. They had been going over one hundred miles per hour on a straight trajectory, already. Residual momentum carried them forward and downward together descending along the latter half of an inverted parabola.

The world splayed before her like a gigantic map, individual farmlands to the north looking like patches on a quilt. The wind was a screaming, laughing thing. It took her a moment to realize the latter laughter came from herself. She was falling, in her head she knew she was, but her body just felt the push of the wind, felt the pull of the straps, and the presence of her man behind her, guiding them down, down, down.

The harness was better than bondage ropes or a corset. Hugging, comforting, controlling. The falling part—or gliding, or whatever it was they were doing—that was about loss of control. The two sensations built into an incredible mixture of panic and pleasure, and as Roy wiggled behind her, she caught just enough of the bulge in his pants to push herself further toward another climax.

Suddenly, she was coming at 4000 feet. Free falling into an afternoon delight. She screamed her orgasm into the wind. Her eyes were locked open, watching the world through her goggles, untouched by the raging winds. She felt like she was sliding down a snowy hill on a polished aluminum disc. Speeding, speeding gone.

Roy shifted again, and the straps pulled against her chest, her crotch, and another orgasm washed through her.

The world that was—one where she was worried about bouts and the future, her dreams and her destiny—winked out in importance, as her man guided them toward the steadily expanding patch of earth destined for their feet. She waved her arms, found the action not as easy as she was used to. But the thrill of pushing was fun.

The thrill of falling was amazing.

He would see them down. They would land safely, she knew. And when they did, she would be different thanks to a new perspective.

That was one thing—

Her straps eased a third orgasm from her.

—one thing this sort of activity granted. Perspective. The world was ultimately small; the people and all their problems were smaller still.

Her eyes managed to fix on the altimeter on her wrist. The needle was descending at a steady rate. All according to plan. All according to physics and the NIST-OWM, she supposed, who would monitor such activities and technologies with well-maintained measuring tapes and digital doodads.

She giggled, warm with this experience.

When the needle struck the right number, Roy pulled his cord and the primary chute opened without issue. Their descent arrested for an instant, and a fourth orgasm burst from her. She wanted to turn around. Cuddle close to this man, her fellow, her Roy.

The straps held her stable and fixed.

She was satisfied with that.

For now.

Her body was not quite done, though. They still had a couple of thousand feet to go, and her heart and pussy would have nothing less than coming down fast and hard. She screamed her wild, wonderful emotional overload to the heavens, to the waiting earth below.

Pierced

By Annabeth Leong

My girlfriend is on her back in our bed, stretched and spread for me. I've spent the last while getting her ready and arranged, kissing and stroking her, undressing her, and winding rope around her wrists and ankles. At this point, I always take a moment to stand back and admire her. Now that she can't turn away or scrunch up to hide from me, I can peruse the mysteries of her body at my leisure.

I've been with Josephine long enough that I know her insecurities as well as I know my own, and the funny thing is, they're what I love most about her. The stretch marks along the sides of her breasts, brought about by changes in her weight over the years, take on a spider-silk delicacy against her dark skin that I love to trace with my eyes, fingers, and tongue whenever she lets me. The thickness of her thighs makes for the most satisfying curves, and when I tie her there tightly enough, I can't get enough of the way the flesh flows over the rope. She worries that the crooked line of her nose makes her look too masculine, but I think that it's awesome that she broke it boxing, and I secretly love the hints of masculinity that spice her abundant femininity. Most breathtaking of all, though—and the nexus of much disagreement between us—are the steel barbells through her nipples.

She's ashamed of them these days. Josephine says she got them when she was young and stupid, and a couple times a week she mutters about how she ought to take them out. The only reason she doesn't, according to her, is that after so many years wearing them, she worries about what her nipples would look like without them. I hope she also leaves them in for me.

She knows what they do to me. Before I learned to keep my mouth shut about them, I often told her about how my clit jerks every time I see the outline of them through her bra and how I'll wake up in the night to the cold, hard feeling of them pressed against my back and it's all I can do not to turn in her arms then and there and wake her with an onslaught of sexual attention.

The first time I saw those pierced tits, they inspired a flood of fantasies that banished my dexterity and rendered me speechless. I wanted to suck those barbells, twist them, and tug them. Most of all, I wanted to tie them. I used to lie awake fantasizing about the ways I could trap and attach them and the various predicaments for Josephine that could involve them.

"What are you thinking about?" Josephine murmurs now, and I look away as if she could read the truth in my eyes. She shifts as much as my ropes allow. I know she wants me to look back at her, but I don't think I should tell her what I want to do to her nipples.

Since we got together, I've eased her into

bondage. She likes for me to tie her spread-eagled to the bed and then lick her pussy until she screams. She enjoyed the time I hog-tied her and tickled her until she gasped for air, then fucked her from behind with my strap-on until she was begging for a different reason. For the most part, though, I've kept it light and fun. I'm afraid that my fantasies about her piercings are a little too dark. I'd like to make her nipples hurt, and I haven't yet talked to Josephine about how she would feel about that.

"Erin... You can't leave me like this," Josephine moans. "What are you thinking? You looked like you wanted to eat me alive."

I raise an eyebrow. "Actually," I remind her, "I *can* leave you like this. That's the point, isn't it? I can stare at that pretty body for as long as I want and just make you wait." As long as she doesn't use her safeword, that is, but she knows that as well as I do.

I take note of the small circles she's making with her hips and the way her hands clench above her tied wrists. Sitting on the bed beside her, I run one finger down the side of her face and watch the shivers that spread through her body in its wake. "Something has my little Josephine very turned on, and I'd like to know what it is."

Josephine pouts. "I asked first."

"I'm not the one tied up." I've found that I can't remind her of that fact too often. I get a delicious reaction every single time I point out to Josephine that she's helpless and at my mercy. It's a wonderful thing to introduce a girlfriend to bondage and discover that it really suits her.

She turns her head away from me. Gently, I grasp

the point of her chin and bring her back. We have a staring contest for a moment, her brown eyes mysterious in the dim light of the bedroom. To assert that I'm the one in charge, I handle her as I wait for her to speak, exploring the sides of her body as if I'm grooming a fine horse's flank.

After a few moments, I win. "There was something dangerous about you," she admits. "You looked like you were thinking about doing something... rough. It got me hot."

"How hot?" I'm trying to look cool and dominant, but what she's saying makes my heart pound. My pussy's so wet I'm sure she can smell it. I skip my hand down her body, avoiding her nipples. She doesn't often let me touch them, and if she did let me now, I would lose control.

Instead, I find my way to her cunt. She's very slippery there, enough that my fingers are inside her before I mean them to be. She cries out and clenches around them, and that strong, velvety grip makes my head spin.

"So hot, so hot, so hot." Josephine's chant tells me how aroused she is. I could make her come with the right touch, but I'm fascinated by what's unfolding and so I hold still and wait. "I want you to hurt me," she moans.

My throat goes dry. I lick my lips, struggling to keep my thoughts coherent. "Baby, are you sure?"

"Yes." The word is a whisper, but there's no uncertainty in her voice.

"Now?"

"Yes."

"Maybe we should talk about this later," I tell her. "I could eat you out like I usually do and we could—"

"Now, Erin. Please. I want you to do whatever you were thinking about doing."

"Josephine. You don't know what that was. Maybe I should just spank you for now and—"

"Please."

"I don't think you're going to like it."

"I don't care." Her voice breaks in the middle of that sentence, and I marvel at what is growing in her. In a few months' time, we've gone from tentative experiments with fuzzy handcuffs to her begging me to hurt her.

Maybe as a top I should resist this. The most responsible thing might be to force her to wait. My blood, however, is rapidly flowing out of my brain and into my clit. Images flash before my mind's eye. There are so many things I've wanted to do to Josephine's pierced nipples, and this is the first time I've gotten the opportunity to really play with them.

"All right," I relent. "Remember your safeword, though, baby. Don't forget that you're in control."

"I know," she says.

To test her, I stare into her eyes and bring my fingers to her nipples. Her sensitivity about those barbells has trained me to be cautious about approaching her breasts, but this time I go for them boldly. I grab one breast firmly in the palm of each hand and squeeze the nipples between thumb and forefinger. She mewls, and I can't read whether it's a sound of discomfort or arousal. Very deliberately, I give each barbell a quarter turn—enough to send a clear signal, but not enough to really hurt. Holding that position, I ask Josephine, "Are you still sure? I want to play with these."

She closes her eyes, and I recognize the combination of shame and excitement that can, at the right moments, make for the most potent of all sexual cocktails. “Yes,” Josephine says.

I increase the quarter turns to half turns. She hisses, but her hips rock. “Still sure?”

“Yes.”

“Last chance, baby, and then I’m not going to hold back unless you use your safeword.” I release the twist and change my grip on the barbells. Then I use them to tug her breasts upward. It’s incredibly satisfying to watch the shape of her breasts change, the flesh lifting into two taut cones. I pull until her nipples lengthen and stretch and she gasps again. “Still sure?”

“Oh God! Yes!”

Considering how embarrassed she’s always been about her piercings, the force of her reaction surprises me. I let go of the barbells and gaze at Josephine. She’s moving constantly now, struggling in her restraints. She’s not trying to get away, though. I think if her hands were free, she’d slap them onto her pussy and finger herself to oblivion.

I lean in very close, enough that my open-mouthed breath mists the surface of the steel ball at the end of one of the barbells. “Tell me about these,” I order Josephine. “The truth, this time. Why did you get them? It wasn’t just that you were young and stupid.”

“They turned me on,” Josephine admits at the same moment my mouth closes over the barbell. She gasps and arches up to me, and the moment is everything I dreamed it could be. Her nipple is warm and hard, scrunched by arousal into a taut nub above a fascinating pattern of wrinkles that feels good against the sensitive tip of my tongue. Punctuating those feelings is the steel barbell, which I flick with my tongue until it clatters against the insides of my teeth. I like the experience of soft mingled with hard, and I could toy with this for hours simply for the sake of exploration and the pleasure of interesting contrasts.

It's more than that, though. The barbell gives me leverage. I can grip it with my teeth much harder than I could bite her actual nipple, and then I can use it to tug her this way and that, to control her at a finer level than I can with the thick ropes I've used so far. I like the intimacy and precision of this hold on her. It makes me dizzy to think about how this piece of steel is *inside* of Josephine. I can manipulate it and connect myself to that deep and permanent penetration.

"Tell me why they turn you on." I make sure to use the present tense, not the past as she did. It's clear that the piercings still get her pussy wet.

"I don't know," she says, her voice honestly bewildered. "There's something sharp about them. The pleasure is clearer. It's hard to explain."

"Why wouldn't you let me play with them?" I'm tonguing them enthusiastically now, licking her breast with the big, broad motions a dog would use.

"It seemed weird. People have always thought I was weird."

"You knew I liked them. And you knew I wanted to tie you up. Why would I think it was weird?"

"I hoped you wouldn't. I guess I was waiting. For you to make me tell you." Josephine takes a while getting those words out. She's panting and moaning so much that it's clearly hard for her to make room for speech.

When she finishes her sentence, though, I want to laugh. All this time I've been working toward admitting my fantasies about her nipples, trying to warm her up, and she's been waiting for me to make her confess hers. "No more waiting, baby. Don't worry."

To keep her busy while I go into my rope bag for the paracord I want, I command Josephine to tell me whether she twists her nipples when she masturbates.

"Yes," she says.

"Could you really have taken those barbells out if you use them to make yourself come?"

"I don't know. I never have."

"Because they get you too hot. Not because you're afraid of how your nipples would look without them."

"Yes."

My hands tremble so much that it's hard to get the paracord. There are so many things I want to do to Josephine's nipples that it's hard to choose just one.

"Do you pull them? Twist them? How do you do it?"

"Um..." Josephine seems both hesitant and uncertain of how to describe what she does.

I solve the problem for her by reaching up and pulling the quick release I tied into the restraint on her right wrist. "Show me."

She bites her lip but obeys. She places her hand on her pierced nipple with a practiced surety that sends a surge to my clit. Then she twists it nearly 360 degrees—much farther than I did in my earlier tests.

The effect takes my breath away. A wave of painful pleasure crashes over her face, tossing her head back. Josephine closes her eyes and lets out a moan from the depth of her soul, and then twists her nipple even more. I can't help but put a hand over my clit when I see the whitened skin around the barbell.

"Do you like that?" I need her to admit it for me.

"Yes."

"I don't think that's weird," I tell her. "I think it's sexy." To prove that, I touch her cunt. I'm stunned by how wet she is. She must be soaking an enormous wet spot onto the bed beneath her. Thick evidence of her arousal flows onto my hand as soon as I spread her entrance open.

"Oh God, Erin, I want to come so badly."

With a flash of inspiration, I know which predicament I want to put her in today. The idea is accompanied by a delicious tingle up my spine as I observe how hungry she is for this. I'll get another chance to play with those barbells. This won't be the first time we do this sort of thing now that we've both admitted how much we want it.

"You'll get to come," I tell her, unable to keep the wicked glee out of my voice.

Josephine opens her eyes wide, lifting her head to look at me. "But...?"

"Baby, you'll see. Give me your right hand."

It takes no time to place a single-column tie around her right wrist with the paracord. I wrap carefully to make sure it won't tighten and cut off her circulation when she tugs on it —because I plan to make her tug on it enthusiastically and with desperation.

Then I guide her hand toward her clit. Josephine tries to close the distance all the way, but I stop her just short. "Stay there and don't move."

She moans a protest, but I'm already finishing the

tie, running the paracord from her wrist up to the barbell attached to her right nipple. The cord is thin enough that I can loop it around the balls at either side of the barbell and trust it to stay in place.

Josephine gasps, and I think she's figured out what I'm going to have her do.

I tug gently to test my handiwork, then pull my hands back. "Okay, sweetie. *Now* you can touch your clit."

Her eagerness to obey belies the whining sound she makes. Josephine extends her hand toward her clit, and the gesture pulls the paracord taut, just as I intended it to. She can't reach her clit without pulling the barbell attached to her nipple.

I watch in fascination as she experiments, learning the limits of the tie. I can see by her winces and gasps that rubbing her clit requires stretching her nipple far enough to hurt, but the fervor of her continued attempts make it equally clear that the pain is stoking her arousal.

My pulse beats in my clit with the force of a hammer. I've never seen anything as hot as Josephine willing to torment her own nipple for the sake of an orgasm. I want her even more wound up, absolutely wild with need, and so I slide one finger into her cunt and wiggle it slightly, enough to tease but nowhere near enough to satisfy her. I stroke her inner walls gently but avoid all her favorite spots.

"Erin! I need it!"

"Show me how much you need it, Josephine."

She throws her head from side to side on the pillow and works her clit harder and faster. The motions make her breast jump, and I love the way that soft, brown flesh ripples and rolls but can't escape the restraint of the paracord and the barbell. I lay a finger against the side of her breast to feel its heat and motion.

"Please! The other one!"

I let out a hiss of my own. This morning, I wouldn't have dared to dream about this scene, and now Josephine is yanking on one piercing as she gets herself off while begging me to play with the other. I hold the barbell firmly and move it in a circle, making her breast swish from side to side beneath it.

The closer she gets to coming, the more frantically she moves. Her body is pulled taut as the paracord, and she grunts and struggles, absolutely lovely in her frenzy. The scents of her body—sweat and pussy and grapefruit soap—go straight to my head. I need to come, too.

I place one hand beside Josephine to hold myself up and climb astride her thigh. I'm still dressed, but I don't have the patience to deal with clothing. I ride her bound body while she jerks beneath me, so caught in the pursuit of her own pleasure that she can't respond to me. I'm still holding her pierced nipple, and as I get closer to coming myself, I tug it harder and harder.

"It hurts!" Josephine wails, but follows that immediately with another cry. "More!"

That's too much for me. I pull her nipple, grit my teeth, and roll my clit over her thigh. Orgasm bursts from me, and I can barely see. I can only feel Josephine, still straining and groaning beneath me. She's lost in need, continuing to masturbate through my orgasm and beyond it. I lower myself onto her body and stare at her breast as it rocks and jiggles from her force.

Then Josephine goes stiff and I know she's found her orgasm. My paracord tugs her nipple down toward her clit, folding it over her breast, and she lets out three sharp cries. I dart my tongue out to lick it, and feel the shudder that passes through her.

"Erin," she sighs, and takes her hand off her clit and places it against the back of my head. Her breast, now released, returns to the position dictated by gravity, still rippling slightly. "Thank you."

"You have no idea how long I've wanted to do that."

"I'm glad you didn't think I was weird."

I stroke the side of her face and offer her a smile. "Baby, you might think *I'm* weird by the time I'm through. That was only the first of many, many ideas."

Josephine grins back, and I see something opening in her face. I rest one finger on the barbell through her right nipple, stroking gently to soothe the irritated flesh around it.

"I'm not going to think it's weird," she whispers.

I flick my gaze up and down her body, taking in the paracord that's still attached to her, and my ties at her ankles and left wrist. She's taken everything I've given and then some, and I realize that she's not the only one who's been insecure. I've been holding back my fantasies, too, certain that she would react badly if I admitted them to her. The tingle lingering in my clit after my orgasm, however, has a very different story to tell.

I've tried so hard to convince Josephine that I adore every part of her, especially those piercings and all the other things that make her feel insecure. Now I see that she's been doing the same for me. I kiss her right nipple, and she sighs. I know she understands.

Wild Cards: Collared & Cuffed
By Del Carmen

Her man was in the backyard putting their black and white pit bull Biggs through his exercises. Ivette still couldn't't believe that she was living out her fairy tale: great job at a five-star hotel, a home in Brooklyn with a decent yard, a good man – in and out of bed - and a wedding next month. She'd just come from her bridal shower, a private lunch with her three BFFs – Laura, Mercedes and Vita. They called themselves the Wild Cards.

Guess she was going to have to give up her title, but then again with all the toys and, of course, the mandatory *Fifty Shades of Grey* "kit" she just got, the wild part would still be true!

She stepped out onto their small porch with a grin on her face. Rey was tossing Biggs a Frisbee. The 90-pound dog jumped high and caught it between his jaws.

Ivette was impressed at the catch, but more so at Rey's muscled torso. She loved him in his business suits, but casual home was a great look too – muscle shirt damp with sweat hugging his abs, low-rise sweats, bare feet and what she noticed to be a notable hard-on.

Rey turned towards her as she walked down to greet him and Biggs, a wide grin on his face. It was that sexy smile that had won her over right from the start she thought, as he tossed the Frisbee to Biggs again and met her halfway. They shared an open-mouthed kiss, and her pussy clenched and drenched.

She wrapped her arms around his waist as their tongues met and danced in and out of each other's mouth. Ivette sunk into the kiss, the warmth of his embrace and the musk of him seducing her when a hard head punched into her crotch and it wasn't Rey.

With both hands she pushed Biggs' head away, and greeted him with a gentle rub.

"Why does he always do that?" she asked.

Rey chuckled and pulled the pit bull away.

"My boy knows where to find the honey pot, and he's not the only one."

Rey wiggled his eyebrows making them both laugh, and Biggs barked in companionship.

They moved as a unit back to the stairs. Rey picked up a discarded towel off the picnic table to reveal a juicy ham bone. He gave the dog a command, that had him sitting up and still. He extended the bone which Biggs took gently from his hand, then made a dash to his favorite sunny spot to gnaw on it.

"How was the lunch?" Rey dropped the towel and dog collar on the kitchen counter, and reached to look in the bags she had brought home.

"It was fun. I brought you back a little of everything."

"So I see." Rey pulled out a penis-shaped chocolate lollipop.

Ivette grabbed it from him.

"That one is for me. There's another one in there for you."

He raised another lollipop, this one shaped like breasts, white with pink nipples.

"I like," he said before licking it.

She licked at her lollipop too. When she saw the answering grin on Rey's face, she bit the tip off her penis and watched the white chocolate breast pop right out of his mouth.

"Witch." His hand curved around her round hips, as he pulled her in for a kiss.

It was a full body kiss. His mouth covered hers, their tongues mated. Hungry. Insatiable. His hands cupped her ass, lifting her up towards his hard dick. She rocked against his hardness while his tongue moved in and out of her mouth.

They came up for air. He rubbed his nose against her cheek breathing in her scent, vanilla and spices. She caressed his cheek with hers, loving the roughness of his five o'clock shadow on her skin.

"What other toys did you get?" He pressed a kiss on her shoulder.

She invited him to take a look, as Rey emptied the bags on the table.

"Can I get you anything?" she asked.

"Maybe later," he replied.

She was putting the food in the fridge, when he snorted behind her. He held up a box with an edible bikini.

"That is for you," she said.

The shocked look on his face was priceless.

"Now this," he stressed, "is more my style."

He examined the nipple clamps, blindfold, feather

tickler and handcuffs. He shook the box that read *Fifty Shades of Grey* kit.

Ivette shook her head.

"Don't ask."

"Take your pick." Rey requested.

She had laughed with the girls when they had spread the items before her. But now in front of her lover, disturbing and delicious thoughts ran through her mind.

"What makes you think they are to use on me?"

He looked perplexed at her question, then intrigued.

"Are you game, lover?" she teased.

"Be gentle with me," he smiled as he handed her the handcuffs.

She twirled them on her fingers, running her eyes over his body.

"You could tie me to one of the posts on the bed," he volunteered.

"Or I can tie you to one of the posts on the kitchen chair," she countered.

He looked bemused.

"I could ride you better," she explained.

"I am all for that!" he exclaimed.

They laughed, adjusting the handcuffs to fit his wrists. The click of the cuffs was loud in the kitchen. They stared at one another, their roles were reversed. Not that Ivette was shy in bed, but they'd never tried anything this racy before. BDSM lite for them…so far.

"First time for everything," Rey said, reading her thoughts. "Now hurry up and have your wicked way with me, woman!"

On a whim, she grabbed Biggs collar off the counter. It fit Rey just fine.

"How do I look?"

"You look good collared and handcuffed, all tied up and all mine."

She straddled him. They rubbed noses, as she ran her hands across his chest.

"You're all sweaty." She licked the salt off his skin, raising his muscle shirt to lick at his nipples.

"Uncuff me so we can take it off," he said.

"Sorry, *querido*, you are staying put." She gave him a quick kiss, before stepping behind him.

He tried to turn without success.

Ivette came back with scissors, and cut his shirt. She looked at his pants.

"Not the pants!" he cried.

"Those I can pull off." She proceeded to do just that. Now she had a naked man tied to her kitchen chair, and at her mercy.

She loved it.

She walked around him. Ran her hand through his hair. Traced the collar, tugging it a little. Then she kissed his neck, shoulders, and ran her hands up and down his strong arms.

She could see that Rey relished the sensation. Even as intimately as she knew his body in the two years they'd been lovers, it felt like she was learning him anew.

"Let me have a lick?"

"You want your lollipop again, lover?"

"I want you."

"I am all yours." She stepped between his legs, pulling her sundress off. She wore a red demi-cup bra that pushed her girls together and provided great cleavage, plus a matching thong. He leaned forward to kiss her stomach, and the underside of her breast.

"Take them out," he asked.

"If you can take them out, they're yours," she challenged moving closer to him, aching for his mouth on her.

He used his teeth to pull at her bra, pushing at it with his nose but settling for sucking her nipples through the satin. She laughed at his frustration, feeling empowered, pretty, witty and gay.

Ivette felt like dancing.

"Hold everything." She grabbed his face with one hand, and puckered his lips to give him a quick kiss. "We need music." She went into the living room, and soon the sexy sounds of guitars filled the air.

Ivette grabbed the feather tickler from the table, swaying it in front of Rey in time to the music. She ran the feather tickler across her face, and down her neck. Her eyes meeting his, she turned to shake her booty at him. The feathers felt soft and velvety against her collar, her breasts, her stomach, her back.

Rey watched her closely, as she lifted one leg and placed her foot on the chair underneath his erection. She wiggled her toes tickling his dick, and felt him pressing down on them.

With her legs parted, she ran the feathers across her wet thong. She ran it up and down her crotch, basking in the heat of his gaze. He couldn't take his gaze off the feathers, as she was got weter and weter. She ran the feathers across her inner thighs, first one, then the other. Rey's cock was at full attention, and weeping for release.

Ivette reached out with the feather, and tickled the

tip of his dick. Their juices mingled on the feathers, she brought it back and ran it against her pussy.

"Damn woman, get over here!"

She laughed.

"Now!" he demanded.

She laughed harder.

"Sorry, querido. *You* are the one collared and cuffed, and at my beck and call."

Ivette ran the feathers across his face, letting him breathe in the scent of their joint arousal. He growled, straining forward.

She wiggled her toes against his dick again, but she had better ideas on how to torture him. When pulled her foot away, Rey protested,

"Hey. I liked it there!"

"I have something better for you," she promised.

Ivette leaned back on the table and spread her legs, pushing her thong aside and slipped two fingers into her pussy.

She heard Rey gasp.

She watched his eyes darken with desire as she played with herself: opening up her lips. spreading her juices around and thrusting her fingers in and out until they were slick with passion. Ivette held her fingers out to Rey.

"Lick," she ordered.

Rey took her fingers eagerly into his mouth, licking them clean.

"Good boy."

"Do I get a treat now?"

"What?" She tilted her head.

"Whenever Biggs is a good boy, he gets a treat. I should too," Rey stated.

"You have been good," she agreed. "A kiss then."

She bent over him, Her lips almost against his. His mouth opened in anticipation, his tongue at the door to great her.

"You have such beautiful lips," she whispered. "Have I told you how much I enjoy stroking them with my tongue or sucking on them?"

"No." Rey's voice was husky with desire. His mouth reached again for hers, but she knelt in front of him instead.

"There is another part of you that I want to kiss instead. My treat." She lowered her head and took his dick in her mouth. His hips pumped upwards with pleasure.

His come was salty on her tongue. She took as much of him as she could into her mouth. Rey was long and thick, so it always took her a couple of swallows to fit all of him in. She grazed him with her teeth the way he liked and squeezed his balls.

He twitched, as she moved his cock in and out of her mouth. His lust was palpable, he was ripe to come so she pulled away.

"Baby, don't stop." he pleaded.

She smiled, straddling him again.

He lifted his hips to fit his dick in her pussy, but she was still wearing her thong and his other big boy was going nowhere.

"Come on, baby. I've been good." He kissed all the parts of her he could reach - neck, shoulders and the top of her breasts.

"Down boy." She leaned back toward the table to grab another toy. Her hand hovered over the blindfold, but she wanted to look into Rey's eyes as they played for the first time.

The nipple clamps looked small and innocent, with a delicate but sturdy chain. She held them in her hand between them, and they stared at each other.

"I am sure those are for you," he said.

"Tonight is all about you, querido," she said.

Ivette rocked against his dick. Her thong was no help, as her juices spread over them. They were both titillated. She kissed his nipples, rubbed them with her thumb, then her tongue and nipped at them. When she felt him relax, she clipped his nipple with the first clamp.

"Fuck. Fuck. Fuck."

He strained back against the chair, she moved back as well to keep them steady and up right.

She removed the clamp and sucked gently on his nipples to ease the sting, as the blood rushed back.

"Damn," His voice was hoarse.

"Again?" Time stood still as she waited for his answer.

"Again," he agreed as he took a deep breath.

She gave him a tongue kiss. Wrapping her arms around his neck, just like her legs were wrapped around his waist. Her wet pussy pressed against his hard abdomen, as she licked and sucked on his lips as she had done on his nipples. His hard dick rubbed against her soft folds.

Ivette pinched his nipples three more times. First one, then the other, each time for a longer period. She had to unleash the chain, as there was not enough length to reach from one of his nipples to the other. He gritted his teeth, blowing out the pain.

"Here's your treat." She stood, removing her bra and thong and offered him her breasts.

He clamped on to her nipple, laving and sucking.

Pulling and biting her hard. She welcomed the pain, welcomed his roughness and his intensity.

He feasted.

She ran her hands across his face. After two years together, she was still surprised that this sexy hunk was all hers.

"Off."

She released the clamps slowly, and rubbed his pebbled nipples as he took gulps of air.

Her man definitely deserved a treat.

She sat on his knees, grabbing his cock. Giving it a few hard pumps, she positioned it at the entrance of her pussy and lowered herself onto his thick staff. The walls of her vagina stretching to accommodate his girth, as she rode him long and hard.

Her ass bounced on his knees, his hips pumping upward to meet her thrusts. They knew each other's rhythms well, as the scent of their fucking filled the air around them.

His cock twitched.

Her clit clenched.

They shivered and cracked under the force of their orgasm. Ivette missed having Rey's arms around her when she came. This time she was doing the holding for both of them.

Later they cuddled in their brass bed, arms and legs entwined.

Bigg snored on his bed in the corner.

Ivette smiled at her good fortune, but she had to know.

"You ok?" she asked.

"Yes." He ran his arm down her back in reassurance.

She hugged him hard. "I liked it."

"Me too." Rey shifted to look at her in the eyes. "But next time more treats and a longer chain for the clamps."

Ivette smiled as she rolled over on top of her man.

What Isn't Necessary Is
By Tomio Hall-Black

"I just don't understand why it's necessary," Katy whispered, running her fingertips over my chest. "We both know that you will let me do anything I want. Why spend the time and effort tying up a willing victim?"

I smiled and cuddled her naked body against mine. A few months ago, Katy had dismissed the idea of bondage without comment. As with so many things concerning her growing control of our sexual relationship, she had allowed it to percolate under the surface until it reached a point where she was ready to deal with it. She was asking for my input, and I knew that after I had offered her whatever she needed to know, she would make an appropriate decision.

"I don't ever consider myself your victim," I said, lifting my head to kiss her mouth softly. "We are partners, we both want this. That's why it works."

She smiled.

"Yes, we both want it. But I still don't understand what we gain by tying you up. Isn't it just as easy to tell you to be still and expect obedience?"

I closed my eyes.

"It's easy, and you know I will do my best to obey, always. But sometimes there might be things other than obedience that are important. Being bound can take us somewhere that we can't get otherwise."

Jess nuzzled against my ear and whispered.

"Oooo – a destination! Poughkeepsie? Albany? Oh, I know! Nova Scotia!"

I laughed along with her. I turned towards her and wrapped my arms around her.

"Try to get away," I whispered.

She looked into my eyes, and slowly arched an eyebrow.

"Please," I said, smiling. "I want to demonstrate something."

"I didn't know I was getting a show, too," she said. Then she put her hands against my shoulders and pushed. I tightened my grip.

Katy twisted and tried to turn. She brought her knee up into my groin. I twisted my hips so that my thigh blocked her and pulled her against my chest. She sank her teeth into my shoulder, and pressed her hands against my face. I groaned in pain, but squeezed her even tighter.

"Okay, you've made your point" she said, a note of frustration finding its way into her voice. "You're bigger and stronger than I am. Didn't we already know this?"

I caught her hands and pulled them down to her sides, then I hugged her even tighter. She growled. It wasn't fun for her. I rolled over on top of her.

"Are you scared, Katy?" I asked.

She went still and looked up at me.

"Of course, not," she said. "You would never do anything to hurt me. You love me."

"Yes, I love you," I whispered, releasing her and

kissing her throat. "I love you enough to lie still and let you indulge the wicked desires that frighten you." I rose up enough to look down into her eyes. "But as long as the only thing that holds me down is my obedience, I will never be scared of what you are doing. I know I can stop it at any time. I will never be pushed to accept anything close to my limit."

"I'm not comfortable pushing things that far," she said, lifting her hands to stroke my cheeks. "I love you, and I enjoy hurting you…but I'm so afraid that I will do something that will injure you or injure what we have."

I turned my mouth to kiss the palm of her hand.

"Whether you push me hard enough to injure or not isn't really the question," I said. "It isn't even the goal. The goal is to put me into a place where I don't know if you are or not, and where I can't do anything about it if you do."

"It's about you not knowing…" she whispered.

"It's about me not having to control myself, and truly having to trust you to be in control," I stroked my hands up and down her naked back. "I know you are scared of some of the things you want to do to me, but I'm not. I know you, and I trust you to know how much I can endure safely."

Katy didn't say anything. She just rolled me off of her and curled up in my arms. She hadn't said yes, but she hadn't said no. I just had to give her the space she needed to consider it. I trusted her. I listened to her breath deepen and held her until I found sleep.

***

I leaned over the foot of our bed, and stretched my arms out in front of me. My feet were spread as far as I could comfortably hold them, and my knees bent slightly. I closed my eyes and leaned my forehead against the down comforter, feeling the cool air on my naked body. This is what Katy expected when she had told me to "assume the position and wait."

I took a deep breath and found my submissive space – that spot deep in my mind where I could let go and not worry about what happened next. It was like sitting in the passenger seat of a car, but much more intimate. Katy was going to drive me somewhere, but only she knew the details. To get there, I had to just…let it happen.

I flinched when Katy's hand brushed against my hip. A deep breath was all it took to find my stillness again. I had been so focused inward, that I hadn't heard Katy come into the bedroom. Now I opened my senses so I could feel her standing behind me, not quite touching me. The warmth of her hand on my hip slid up over my back, and was joined by a matching warmth as both hands moved back down.

"We're going to do something new tonight," Katy said softly. "I want you to remember that I love you, and while I'm going to enjoy hurting you, I will never truly harm you. You are safe."

I nodded, my face rubbing against the comforter. I felt Katy's hands leave my back, and the air felt even cooler than before. The bed moved as she climbed onto it, sliding a length of cloth under my face so that it covered my eyes and tied it behind my head. Her lips were close enough to my ear that I could feel the whisper of her lips as she spoke to me.

"It's okay to be scared tonight," she told me. "I love you."

I heard a soft jingling as a band of leather was closed around my wrist, and pulled tight. Then the other wrist was cuffed as well. There was a bit of pulling and another jingle or two as Katy fastened them together. My heart began to race as I realized what she was doing. I focused on my breathing, keeping my body relaxed and under control. I didn't want to tense and make her think something was wrong. So I just trusted her, and let her continue.

Since I was blindfolded, I couldn't tell what Katy was doing exactly. There was the sound of a metallic click between my wrists, followed by a series of tugs. The bed bounced a bit as Katy moved around, and my wrists were suddenly pulled forward as far as I could reach. There was a bit more tugging, and I heard Katy muttering something I couldn't quite make out. Then she bounced off of the bed and it was quiet.

A few seconds later, a leather strap was fastened around my ankle and tugged towards the bedpost. Then the other ankle was given the same treatment. My feet were a bit further apart than was comfortable and my arms pulled forward far enough that I felt off balance, but I took a deep breath and accepted it. This was part of her controlling things. It wasn't going to be exactly the same as when I did it on my own. That was the point.

Katy's mouth was next to my ear again.

"I have some music for you to listen to," she whispered. "I'm not going to cover your mouth, because I want to be able to hear you if you need something." She bit my earlobe softly. "I also want to hear you beg for more." She giggled softly and a pair of headphones was shoved down over my ears. A second or two later, Lady Gaga demanded that I show her my teeth, and the bass began thumping against the back of my brain. Then Katy turned the volume up enough that it was sure to drown out any sound she made.

I felt a leather belt slither across my back. My heart raced in anticipation of the first stroke, but I made myself take long, slow breaths. Katy's hand traced lightly from my shoulders, down past my ribs, to my hip. I was totally unprepared for the first bite of the belt.

It fell like a flash of fire between my shoulder blades. With the music pumping in my ears, I couldn't hear the pop of the leather. I couldn't hear the whistle of it racing towards my flesh. A second flash seared across my back, making an X between my shoulders. I huffed my breath through my nose, seeking the headspace where I could accept this pain.

Trust her, I told myself. Be strong. You are loved.

There was no use in counting how many times I was hit, because I knew that Katy was the ultimate counter. I opened and closed my hands and waited. The belt fell in a regular rhythm. Each stripe on my skin was almost on top of a previous stripe, so the fire began to build across my skin. I bowed my back upwards as much as I could to offer Katy as a vulnerable target. She took advantage of it mercilessly.

I thought I moaned with each blow, but I couldn't hear it. The music had changed to a dance tune with no words, just a driving energy that pushed me into a sensory-deprived overload. The belt was concentrated on the sweet spot between my shoulders, just under the base of my neck. Katy knew that I could accept a lot of punishment, and she wasn't holding back.

I began to say her name over and over again, a single word of thanks and acceptance for this amazing gift. Katy stopped for a moment, then lifted one side of the headphones to whisper, "I bought a flogger today. It's going to hurt." Then she returned me to the throbbing electronic maze in my ears.

The pain became sharper. The tails of the flogger bit into a dozen different places, then slowly stroked from my shoulders to my hips. I bit the comforter, and clenched my teeth into it. This was a new type of pain, and I didn't know how to accept it freely. Katy didn't give me the chance to adjust, she just rained blow after blow on my back. I panted and gasped, but heard nothing of my own suffering. I tugged at the bonds on my wrists, which held me in place.

I jumped when Katy draped a rope over my back, just above my hips. I could tell it was rope because it was thick and heavy enough, that I felt the braided strands against my skin. Then it was pulled tight, and my back arched downwards. A few moments of tugging, pulling and more tugging and my entire torso was trapped against the bed. Katy patted my ass cheek gently.

There was no warning before my ass became Katy's target, no whistle or thwack. All I could hear was Nickleback: "I like your pants around your feet/I like the dirt that's on your knees." I guessed that Katy was using the riding crop I had given her for her birthday, because it hit hard and fast, and stung like a thousand angry bees. I panted and whimpered into the bed, but I couldn't twitch my hips away from her assault.

Be strong, I thought. Accept it. Do it.

As suddenly as it began, the spanking stopped. There was a tugging at my wrists and I thought Katy was going to release me, but then the bonds were pulled tight again. A few seconds later, my feet were pulled apart even further. Then Katy reached between my legs and squeezed my balls in her palm. When I didn't react, she squeezed even harder until my hips tried to wiggle away. My thighs trembled a bit when she held my balls between her palms and squeezed with both hands.

Katy had hurt my balls before. In fact, she loved to do it right before she allowed me to come. But it was usually a short squeeze, just enough to make me gasp. This squeeze was relentless and hard enough that I fought to curl up. I was helpless. She rolled her hands slowly, until I began to wonder how long I could take it.

As soon as she released my balls, the spanking began again. The flogger had been replaced by something longer, harder and heavier. It stung, and shoved the burn deeper into the flesh of my exposed ass. All I could hear was electronica mix promising to "make you cry…make you scream…" I began sobbing softly, but I couldn't even it.

It was an amazing experience, to be thrashed and yet be completely separated from what was happening. Katy stopped and ran her hands over my ass and my back, admiring her work and reassuring me. I couldn't stop crying, but I begged her to not be done with me. If she answered me, I couldn't hear it. I was in my own world.

I was sure it was over. Katy had always kept well back from my limits, to the point where I had grown cocky about being able to take anything she handed out. I wasn't beyond my limits, but I was close enough to not know how much more I could take. Then I felt a well-lubricated and gloved hand reach between my legs and slowly stroke my cock which was half-hard already, and Katy knew how to tease it perfectly. Soon it was achingly hard, and I wanted to thrust into her hand. But I was helpless, and Katy was in no rush to let me go anywhere. I felt my legs quiver as she let my excitement build. She released my cock and squeezed hard on my balls so that I pulled on my restraints. In my mind, I could almost hear her laugh at my frustration, and that only made me want it more.

Still pumping my cock slowly, Katy pushed two of her fingers into my ass, and pressed her thumb up between my legs. She found my prostate and squeezed it, I shuddered, shivered and gasped. I felt gobs of fluid dripping from my cock, Katy was relentless. Even after I was sure that I was empty, she kept squeezing and stroked my prostate. She pushed me to the edge and then milked my prostate; then pushed me to the edge again.

Her fingers left me, and I panted in relief. Then Katy slipped a toy inside of me that curled between my legs like a C. The ends of it pinched together so that my prostate was still squeezed tightly. When it started vibrating, I whimpered and I felt my thighs shake.

Now both of her hands were free to torment my cock and balls again, and she made good use of that freedom. She tugged my balls downward with one hand, and spanked them with the other. All the while, the buzzing on my prostate pushed tiny drops of fluid out of my cock. She only stopped hurting my balls long enough to push me to the edge, and there was absolutely nothing I could do about it.

As suddenly as it began, everything was over. Katy's released my cock and balls and the buzzer was slipped out of my ass. After a minute, a warm, wet cloth was used to clean me off, and Katy slowly stroked every inch of my ass and back. I managed to stop crying at some point, when Katy removed the headphones.

She didn't say anything, or maybe my ears were just ringing loudly enough that I didn't hear her. The bed shifted, and the warm lusty scent of Katy's pussy hit my nose as I felt her body stretch out over my extended arms. I didn't need instructions when she grabbed a handful of hair and pressed my face against the creamy wetness of her excitement. I shivered and whimpered when her riding crop popped against my ribcage, but I focused on finding the place that made her shiver in delight. After all I had taken tonight a few swats weren't going to phase me.

After the mind-numbing sound of music, the silence of Katy's thighs pressed against my ears was deafening. I couldn't hear all her little sighs and panting noises. I could tell from the way her thighs were squeezing that she was close, and the way her hips shoved up tight against my mouth told me she was hungry. It wasn't until she shuddered, and fell back in bliss that I was able to hear a soft murmur of her pleasure.

The tautness holding my arms was suddenly gone. Katy rolled to one side and fumbled with the clasps that held the cuffs on my wrists. When they were separated, she pushed them away gently.

"Can you get free now?" she asked, her voice slurred with pleasure. "I really don't want to move right now."

I curled my arms around her hips, and pulled her slick pussy back to my mouth. Thrusting my tongue as deep as I could reach, I lapped at her creamy goodness. She giggled and ran her fingers through my hair.

"You can do more of that," she said. Then she gasped and pumped her hips as I ran my tongue over her clit. "Yes. More of that." She pointed a finger between her legs for emphasis. "More of that."

I closed my eyes and let my tongue adore her. It was an odd experience as my legs were still pulled wide and tied to the bedposts, and the rope around my waist held me against the bed. But my upper body was free to reach for her, and I buried my face in her, giving her all of the love and adoration I could manage to put into the swirling, flicking, slurping dance of my tongue.

This time I heard Katy moan and pant. Her hips urged me faster and her hand shoved me tightly against her pelvis. Then she went rigid and made no sound for several seconds before moaning loudly and shuddering. I gave her time to catch her breath, gently lapping her juices from her soft folds.

I had begun to wonder if Katy had forgotten I was still tied to the bed when she finally rolled over and slid off of the bed. The rope around my waist went slack, and she released my ankles. My inner thighs protested, but it was worth it. Katy draped her body over the top of mine and kissed my back.

"Come to bed, my love," she said softly. She

moved over a bit so she wouldn't climb over me and pulled herself up on the bed. I followed her until my mouth was even with her breasts. Wrapping my arms around her, I closed my mouth around her nipple and suckled gently. Katy sighed, and held me against her body.

Katy found sleep first, her breath coming deep and even as I curled into her. Eventually, I drifted off to sleep too, holding the woman I loved with leather cuffs still fastened to my wrists and ankles. It wasn't necessary to keep them on, but I liked the way they felt.

Charlene's Surprise
By Daily Hollow

"Honey, what's the old wooden chair doing in the living room?" Joel asked, rubbing his sore feet. The baseball game was on, and he was *really* looking forward to relaxing.

"Long day?" Charlene asked.

Joel gave her a brief kiss.

"Long's an understatement," he sighed. "Ever since my promotion, I've been working through lunch."

"Well Mr. Director of Marketing, the paycheck's certainly better."

"I know that's right," Joel agreed, returning his attention back to the living room.

"What *is* that old thing doing in there? I thought we sold that sucker on Craigslist a long time ago?"

His wife smiled and said, "I can tie better knots in that chair."

"Knots?"

"Yeah, knots."

Joel closed his eyes as their lips again met.

"Why would you want to tie knots *in* the chair?" he asked when his wife pulled away.

"Because we're going to take your clothes off, and I'm going to tie you up."

"Um...on that?"

"Yup," she replied. "I want to give you a special show to celebrate your recent promotion."

"What kind of show?" He was a little curious since it had been a while since they had done anything wild and crazy.

"You'll see." She winked, then removed his tie.

"This would make a good blindfold," she said, examining the silk fabric. "However, later tonight, now I'm going to need your full attention."

Joel unbuttoned his shirt as his wife pulled his pants and boxers around his ankles, then led him to the living room where she instructed him to sit. She left briefly, then returned with a few pieces of rope.

"You're *really* going to tie me up?"

"That's the plan, darling. Now sit down and be still." Once he complied, Charlene bound his ankles.

"Put your arms on the arms."

"Arms on the arms?" Joel laughed.

Charlene chuckled.

"Just do it, babe."

Joel did as instructed. Charlene went to work, securing his wrists, forearms and elbows.

"Comfy?"

"As comfy as a man tied naked to a chair can be."

She had done a fantastic job with the rope. He couldn't move his arms or ankles.

"Did you learn these knots in the Navy?"

Charlene nodded, then chuckled.

"That chair looks like it could get a little wobbly. Try not to get *too* excited."

"I'll try," he said. "But a lot depends on what you have in store."

She winked.

"You'll see."

Joel looked down at his semi-hard cock, which seemed to share his curiosity.

"I'm going to leave you alone a sec," she said, sashaying from the room.

As Charlene made her way up the stairs, Joel looked around for possible hints. He briefly considered some sort of striptease, but that would be too obvious. His wife was anything but cliché.

Joel tested the ropes again, but could only move his knees and thighs. When he tried to lift his ass, he only rose a few inches from the seat.

He looked up at the clock–it was just after seven. The Red Sox were on at eight.

Moments later, Charlene returned naked--her long, blonde hair falling over her small, lovely breasts.

"Wow," he said, staring at her crotch. "I see you mowed the lawn."

"I had a little help," she purred.

"Um…what?"

Joel heard someone descend the stairs. Seconds later, Charlene's good friend Xanthia entered the living room in just her bra and panties. She had a small dragonfly tattoo just below her bellybutton and her large brown nipples were visible beneath the thin fabric.

"Hi, Joel," she said, nonchalantly. "Nice cock."

"Char, uh…what's going on here?"

"Xan and I are going to put on a little show," she said, walking toward the coat closet. "I sold three houses this week, and Xanthia's paintings are selling at a record pace. We're *all* celebrating."

Charlene opened the door. Standing on her tiptoes, she reached for something on the top shelf. Joel swallowed as her firm ass tightened.

"Oh…my…God," he said. Charlene held a large sex toy. His dick went from curious to rock-hard.

"Do you know why it has two rounded ends, honey?" she asked him.

Joel licked his lips, and nodded.

"Shall we start ass-to-ass?" Xanthia asked.

Joel turned toward his wife's friend as she stepped out of her panties, revealing her razor-thin strip of dark pubic hair.

"Sure, why not," Charlene answered.

He gasped when Xanthia removed her bra. The black woman's firm breasts sat on her body like a pair of large brown teardrops. Her nipples resembled brown pencil erasers, while her aureolas were nearly the size of coffee coasters.

Joel stared at the double-headed dildo his wife held.

"Char, what are you going to do with that?" he asked, then realized how stupid he sounded.

He took a deep breath as his wife walked toward him, holding the large purple shaft inches from his face.

"What end would you like for me to slide into my wet pussy?" she asked him

He nodded toward her left hand, though it didn't really matter.

Charlene licked the tip of the chosen section, her eyes never leaving his. His Adam's apple bobbed like a monkey on a stick. She gave him another kiss, and then positioned herself on the floor.

"Wait for me," Xanthia said, getting on her hands and knees, her thick brown ass facing Charlene. Joel's eyes widened as his wife slowly guided one end into her pussy, Xanthia took care of the other.

He managed to catch a brief glimpse of pink, before the dildo made its way between their swollen lips. Both women moaned as they slowly backed up toward each other. When their cheeks touched, there was a sexy contrast between his wife's white ass and Xanthia's brown booty. Beads of sweat formed on Joel's brow.

"Fuck," Charlene gasped.

"Yeah, c'mon honey, let's *do* this," her friend encouraged.

"Holy shit," Joel whispered.

They rocked slowly at first, their asses jiggling like vanilla and chocolate pudding, tits swaying back and forth. Five feet away, Joel's view from the side was perfect. Since his wife's backside was much smaller, whenever their asses came in contact, Xanthia's cheeks would spread. Angling his neck, Joel was able to catch a glimpse of the black woman's tight little pucker.

Joel let out a whimper when the sloshing noises began. Moments later he strained against the ropes like a trapped werewolf during full moon.

Since Xanthia was heavier than his wife, her momentum caused Charlene's body to creep forward. Still fighting the ropes, Joel craned his neck in an attempt to maintain his premium view. He shifted his body as they slid further away.

As their asses slammed violently against one another, Joel focused his attention on the slick dildo –

a good portion would come briefly into view, then disappear.

Charlene was the first to come as she screamed his name, then Xanthia's. When the two settled down for a moment, he heard dogs barking. He glanced at the window above the couch, next to Xanthia's painting of the Carolina sunrise.

Fuck, it's open.

While the window faced the woods, the only thing separating their house from the neighbors was a small privacy fence and about fifty feet.

"Do you like that?" Charlene panted as her ass smacked against Xanthia's.

"Uh, huh," she managed.

A few minutes later Xanthia squealed so loud, Joel thought the large mirror in the dining room would shatter. The smell of sex began to spread throughout the room, driving him even crazier. Forgetting the window, he continued struggling with the restraints, wishing his wife hadn't done such a good job.

The two women gradually slowed, eventually coming to a stop. There was burning in his wrists and forearms. When he looked down he noticed they were red from rope burn. His ankles felt like they were on fire as well.

Xanthia noticed something else.

"Looks like your husband *really* enjoyed the show," she said.

"He does look as though he could use a little relief," Charlene said. "Why don't you see what you can do to help?"

Xanthia disengaged herself, slowly crawling toward Joel until her face was inches from his pulsing red knob. He sucked in a breath as she gently blew on its tip.

Charlene stood, revealing two large rug burns on her knees. Nearly a quarter of the sex toy was still lodged inside her.

Joel groaned as Xanthia slowly stroked his cock, causing his toes to curl.

"Get that ass in the air, girl," Charlene ordered as she moved closer, holding the dildo that still protruded from her sex.

Xanthia raised her bottom, as she took Joel in her mouth.

"Jesus Christ," he sighed.

Charlene slid the toy inside her. Xanthia moaned around his cock, sending shockwaves throughout his body. As Charlene's pace quickened, Xanthia's did as well.

"Just like that, Xanthia," Joel gasped as he watched his wife fuck her friend's pussy. Moments later, he shot a several loads into the black woman's mouth. When Joel pulled out, Xanthia looked up, her bottom lip quivering. Soon her eyes rolled back. Joel hissed as her nails dug into his thighs, leaving large U-shaped imprints.

"I'm gonna come," Xanthia panted.

Charlene sped up until her friend cried out. After giving her a few hard thrusts, Charlene stopped.

"What else can we do with this monster?" Xanthia asked once she caught her breath, looking at the dildo.

Joel was a little disappointed she wasn't referring to him.

"Let's get on our asses," Charlene suggested.

Once they were both on the floor facing each other, Charlene slid the dildo into her swollen pussy and eased the other end into Xanthia's. They raised their hips and scooted forward, until the sex toy disappeared. The women lowered themselves back to the carpet, Charlene reached across and teased Xanthia's clit. Moments later, Xanthia returned the favor.

Watching the two beautiful women fuck and play with each other, was enough to bring Joel's cock from at ease to full attention. He continued his losing battle with his wife's handiwork, as the two women leaned forward until their foreheads touched. Charlene's long, sweaty strands fell between them, while Xanthia's shorter hair stayed in place.

As they fucked more passionately, the speed of their thumbs and fingers increased. Xanthia came first, letting out another high-pitched shriek. Moments later, Charlene yelled to God and Jesus. Joel was so horny he would have sucked his own cock if he could have bent far enough.

The two women remained on the floor, panting and sweating. The sex smell intensified, and wet spots dotted the carpet. Charlene crawled toward him. Joel admired his wife's tolerance, since her rug-burned knees likely hurt like hell.

"My turn," she purred.

"Oh, God, Char," Joel gasped as she slowly stroked him.

"Do you want to watch me fuck your wife?" Xanthia asked as she massaged the sex toy against Charlene's pussy.

Joel nodded.

Charlene yelled out as Xanthia filled her cunt. She bucked her hips, trying to match her friend's rhythm, while pistoning her hand along her husband's shaft.

Joel's second orgasm took much longer than the first, but was just as intense. His first load shot past Charlene's head, hitting Xanthia's chin. The next several covered his wife's back, hair, eye and cheek. Charlene licked her hand, while Xanthia continued pounding her with the dildo. Joel wondered how long Xanthia could keep going at that pace before her arm got tired.

Charlene gasped, then moaned as she looked up at Joel. He could tell she was close. A large string of come was tangled in her eyelid, while the gob on her cheek ran toward her jawline.

Still working Charlene's pussy, Xanthia bent down and licked her back clean and began tonguing her asshole.

"Uh…uh…oh!" Charlene screamed as her body shook.

"Just like that!"

"Don't stop!"

"Yesssssss!"

When Xanthia finally removed the dildo, Charlene took a few breaths before slowly turning and licking her friend's chin clean. Xanthia returned the favor by tonguing Charlene's eye, and the side of her face. The two beauties then kissed in earnest.

For the second time in nearly twenty minutes, Joel was spent. He grinned at the two women in front of him.

"Have you enjoyed yourself so far?" Charlene asked after pulling away.

"Oh, hell yeah!"

What the fuck kind of question was that?

She looked at the clock and said,

"The baseball game's about to start. Xan, can you help me turn the chair so Joel can see the television?"

"Absolutely."

They each grabbed a side, and spun him around until he faced the large flat screen. Charlene turned the television on, changing the channel to the New England Sports Network.

"If you two have any more tricks up your sleeves, the game can go to hell," Joel said. For the first time in years he didn't give a rat's ass about Big Pappi *or* the Boston Red Sox.

"We need to take a break," Charlene said.

"Whoa," Joel gasped as clear fluid ran down both women's thighs, while the smell of their arousal dominated the room.

"I say we go out for a few drinks, and plan our next show," Xanthia suggested.

"What a marvelous idea. Don't go anywhere, honey," his wife teased, giving him a peck on the lips.

"Ta-ta for now," her friend added. Joel shivered when Xanthia slowly ran her long nails along his navel.

As they were about to go up the stairs, Joel asked, "Can I get some water?"

"Of course, dear," Charlene said, then headed for the kitchen.

"You have an amazing wife," Xanthia said.

"I sure do," he sighed. "How, uh, long have you two –"

"About three weeks. We've been trying to come

up with a creative way to include you. Once you received your promotion, Charlene called and we brainstormed."

Charlene entered the room with a glass of water, putting the glass to his lips. Joel drank until there was nothing left.

"The window above the couch is open," he said.

Charlene flushed.

"Shit, Jan and Robert probably heard everything," she said.

"Maybe we can invite them sometime," Xanthia suggested.

Joel smiled at the thought of the leggy redhead joining in on the fun.

"Perhaps," Charlene said as she closed the window. "I'm sure we can dig up another chair for Robert."

The ladies then left the room.

The commentators were going over the starting line-ups when the two women walked down the stairs, discussing the latest episode of *American Idol*.

Charlene smiled and said, "Enjoy the game."

"Can you untie me before you go?"

Charlene shook her head.

"Why would we want to do that?"

"Um, I just drank a whole glass of water. Unless you want to come home to more stains on the carpet, I would suggest you set me free."

The two women looked at one another. Charlene sighed, and undid the knots.

Once free, Joel rubbed his arms and ankles.

"Can you grab me a Big Mac on your way back? I *really* don't feel like cooking."

"You should probably save your appetite."

"Why? I'm starved."

Charlene winked.

"A reverse Oreo may be added to the menu tonight."

"Sounds delicious," Xanthia said, wiping a strand of hair from Charlene's face.

Joel thought so, too.

Three Knots
By Mercedes Cruz

After her last final, April felt good about herself since she had studied all semester long and was determined to keep her grades up regardless of her emotional state, so she decided to celebrate with her boyfriend, Marcus.

When she opened the room to his dorm, she found him in bed with Marshall, his freshman tutor.

"April, it's not what it looks like, let me get dressed and we can talk."

Those were the last words she heard from Marcus as he lay naked in bed with another man.

She needed to forget.

April's best friend Monica had an end of the semester party in her dorm room. When she got there, the room was packed: guys, girls, liquor and music blasting from portable speakers. Most of their friends were in the room, including Lenny, Marcus' hot roommate, and his polar opposite.

Lenny flirted with April all night, but she tried to act as if she didn't notice. He played along, as they danced to a few songs. When the party was winding down and people were leaving, Lenny approached

April who was talking to Monica.

"I'm leaving now, Monica, thanks again for inviting me. April, it was good to see you.," he said, lingering even though he said he was leaving.

Monica gave April a wink and a sly grin.

"You're so sweet Lenny, I wish we had more guys on campus like you." Monica's grin widened into a huge smile. "And on that note, it's getting kind of late for my best friend here to walk all by herself across campus back to her dorm. I think you should walk her there."

"Um, I will be fine, don't worry about me," April turned to Monica, surprised and annoyed.

"April, you know I don't mind, I'll wait for you downstairs," Lenny quickly replied.

"What was that about? Why did you ask him to walk me?" April cornered Monica as soon as Lenny left.

"What's wrong? I'm looking out for you, I want you to get home safe and maybe get some!"

"What?"

"Oh come on April, this room was full of hot girls tonight--including me--but Lenny flirted with you all night long."

"What's your point, Monica?"

"Don't play stupid, I know you noticed the way he looked at you."

"Okay, whatever, I have to go."

"Yeah, you don't want to leave Lenny waiting too long. Let me know how it goes!"

"Good night Monica," April said sarcastically, and flicked her hand.

*

"So what are your plans for winter break?" Lenny broke the silence.

"Um, I'm... I'm not sure Lenny."

"Well don't you want to see your family, your friends or just get off of campus?"

"I do, but I don't want to see me friends and family right now after what happened with Marcus..."

"You shouldn't be embarrassed because you're no longer dating him."

April took a deep breath,

"You're right. Still, I just need sometime alone,"

When they arrived at her dorm, Lenny gave April a hug and kiss, which took her by surprise.

"Merry Christmas."

April had a big grin on her face. The feeling of his strong arms around her and the smell of his aftershave, turned her on. She wanted to invite him upstairs, but did not dare to.

"Thanks for walking with me Lenny. Good night," she said instead, wanting to get away quickly.

"Anytime April, anytime..." His voiced trailed after her, as she walked into her dorm building.

April hurried into her dorm room, hoping her roommate was not around. Luckily her dorm room was empty. She quickly grabbed her iPad mini, and got under her covers, typing the address to one of her favorite porn websites. She placed her hand under the cover, bringing her right hand in between her thighs as she watched as the actors slowly taking off each other's clothing. April imagined Lenny taking off her clothing slowly, the smell of his aftershave, his strong arms about her. Just as she started to finger herself, she heard a clicking of the key in the door. It was Fanta, her roommate.

"Shit…" sighed April, quickly turning off her iPad and sitting up in her bed.

The next morning April gathered Marcus' belongings in her room, placing them all into a large black garbage bag. She left the bag in front of his door with a note that read,

Dear Dirty PIG, this belongs to you.

On her way out of the building, she bumped into Lenny. Lenny's sexy dark brown eyes pierced through her, making her melt inside.

"Hi April, were you looking for Marcus? He's not upstairs, I just saw him in the cafeteria with his tutor."

April rolled her eyes, and shook her head.

"Hi Lenny. No I was just dropping some things he left at my place."

"Oh, well if you need a ride into the city, let me know, I'm leaving this afternoon. I know Marcus used to be your ride..."

"That's very kind of you Lenny, but I decided to stay on campus during the break," April said her head low, as if she were embarrassed.

"Are you sure? Listen if you change your mind, just let me know. Let me give you my cell number." Lenny searched his pockets.

April already had two offers for a ride back to the city, but she had no intention of seeing her family. Before she had broken up with Marcus, she was looking forward to introducing him to her grandmother.

April and Fanta were among a handful of students that stayed on campus. The whole week, April's parents spent the whole time calling her, but April would refuse to go home. It was one of the longest weeks ever.

When the break was over, Lenny visited April and Fanta with home -cooked food, his mother had prepared. He invited them out to dinner that night, picking them up that evening and driving to the town's sushi bar. They ate, drank, laughed and had a great time. Fanta and April drank a little too much sake, and on the way back to their dorm in the car April was all over Lenny.

"Damn Lenny, you're really strong. Your muscles are huge," she said, grabbing his right bicep with both her hands.

Fanta sat in the back seat giggling the whole time. Lenny parked the car, walked them to their dorm.

"Aren't you coming upstairs?" asked April, still a little tipsy from her one too many sakes, but fully aware of what she was doing.

"I wasn't planning to?" Lenny replied hesitantly, not sure if he should.

Fanta walked right past them into the dorm, and up to their room.

"Well, maybe you should just for a little bit..." April teased, still all over him.

"Ok, why not!"

They headed upstairs, April with a big grin on her face. In their dorm room, Fanta was already in the bathroom.

April took advantage, tried to make Lenny feel comfortable.

"Can I get you something to drink, soda, water, juice?"

"No, I'm fine, thanks. I don't plan to stay long, I know your roomie Fanta must be sleepy"

"Okay, but I'm sure she doesn't mind. Do you want to watch a movie?"

Lenny gently grabbed her arms and kissed her. April gasped with surprise. Her heart beat rapidly, as she grabbed his hardening cock with both of her hands. She was very sure of what she wanted.

Suddenly they heard footsteps and both of them moved away from each other. The doorknob turned, and both of them took a deep breath. Fanta walked in, with her bright pink bathrobe on. She smiled and waved at Lenny, still a little tipsy.

"I didn't know you were coming up?"

"Ahhh, yeah I just came to drop off something I forgot to give April." Lenny said put on the spot.

April blushed, looking at the bulge in Lenny's pants which was too big to ignore.

"Ok I'm leaving now. Good night ladies."

April and Lenny made plans to meet up again. They went out for dinner and a movie. Afterwards they went back to Aprils' room. Since Fanta had plans, the room would be empty.

As Lenny and April started their rendezvous with soft R&B music playing from April's phone. Lenny hovered above her, shirtless, his pants down to his ankles. April lay beneath him wearing only her matching lace purple thong and bra. As they kissed passionately, Lenny reached over and grabbed a condom from his pants pocket. He unwrapped it, placing it on his rock hard cock. April watched with anticipation. Suddenly then the room was lit up, the lights were on. Fanta had walked in on her cell phone, so she had not noticed what was going on yet, when she put her phone down to hang her coat on the backdoor hook, she turned around and saw them moving around under the covers on Aprils' bed.

"Oh! April I didn't know you were going to have company..." Fanta said nervously.

Lenny popped his head up from underneath the covers

"Don't be sorry, it's my fault, I shouldn't be here. Just give me two minutes, I'm getting out of here."

"Actually you don't have to, I think I want to watch, if you don't mind?" replied Fanta, as she winked at him and crossed her arms.

April popped her head from under the covers.

"What the hell?" She sat up on the bed, using the sheet to cover herself.

"Oh shit, I didn't see that coming!" Lenny grinned from ear to ear.

"Neither did I, but we can blame it on the Pina Coladas I just had. I've never seen live porn before, maybe this can be like porn unplugged or something," Fanta suggested.

"Are you fucking serious?" replied April still in shock.

"Let's do it, April. We're young, horny and she's tipsy. Maybe she won't remember," said Lenny.

"Lenny, you're fucking crazy. No way," replied April.

"You're right April, I'm crazy about you and I'm going to fuck you," he yelled as he pulled back the sheets, revealing his thick, long cock. He gently pulled down April's thong, planted soft kisses from her face down to her throbbing clit. He lifted his head, and looked directly into her eyes as he slowly entered her. Lenny stroked her in and out, as Fanta stood and watched them.

Lenny choked a strangled groan as he came.

That weekend the trio planned a date. They went out for dinner, came back to the room for an expanded rendezvous. This time no one was drunk and Fanta joined in the fun. Lenny grabbed a small leather tote from the backseat, and they hurried to the dorm room. Locking the room before taking each other's clothing off like savages, Lenny stopped halfway while pulling the sleeves off of April's tight dress.

"Do you remember when I said I wanted to try something new with both of you?" Lenny whispered as he grabbed both the ladies close to him.

Lenny removed April's clothing one piece at a time: first her lacy dress, then her purple bra and left only her lace thong. He grabbed one of the wooden chairs in the room and moved it to the center of the room.

"I want you to sit here," he instructed April, pointing to the chair.

Fanta and Lenny tied one rope around April's mouth with a ball gag, the second around her ankles, and a third knot around her wrists. He caressed April's cheek, before fondling her nipples while sucking and nibbling on her earlobes. His hand moved between her thighs, and he pulled back her thong slipping in one finger and then another, stroking his fingers steadily in and out of her. He brought his hand up to his mouth, and sucked each finger one by one.

Lenny turned to face Fanta, who was seated quietly on her bed watching Lenny's every move. Lenny slowly took off Fanta's blouse, and Fanta helped him take off his shirt. Lenny sucked alternately on Fanta's nipples, before instructing her to play with his hardening cock.

"You have to make it harder," he stated.

"How do you want me to do that?" she teased.

"Play with it, use both your hands to stroke it up and down."

Lenny got up, walked over to his leather bag and took out another rope. He stood in front of Fanta as she sat on the edge of the bed

"Put your arms out straight," he instructed.

She did, and he tied her wrists together.

"I want you doggy style--face down ass up," he stated pointing to the middle of the bed, and slapping her ass.

Lenny returned to April who was trying to talk, but could not be understood through the ball gag. He gently removed the gag from her mouth. As she sat panting and choking, he waited until she composed herself and pushed his tongue down her throat.

"Are you having fun yet?" He paused and whispered into her ear.

"Yes, yes," she nodded as waves of ecstasy ran through her body.

Lenny joined Fanta who was waiting her turn on the bed, propped up on her tied wrists, head down and her butt in the air. Lenny spread her thighs as much as he could, then slapped each butt cheek once. He spread her butt cheeks, and placed his face between them, licking her ass crack, and then her cherry sucking on it like a Popsicle.

"Ahhh… Oh my God, oh my goodness. Yes, Yes..." moaned Fanta.

Lenny stood on the bed, squatted and entered Fanta, stroking her as hard as he could.

As April watched them from the wooden chair

she was tied to, her eyes widened, her mouth watered, her nipples hardened and her thong was now soaked. Lenny and Fanta finished with both of them coming at the same time. Lenny than got up from the bed with his condom still on, and untied April's knots.

"This was the best date ever!" stated Fanta.

"Are you OK, April?" asked Lenny, caressing her face.

"I'm more than okay," replied April taking short deep breaths in and out, biting her lower lip.

Trying something kinky and out of her comfort zone was just what April needed to feel like a new woman. It made her able to forget her romance with Marcus, and think about her erotic potential with Lenny and surprisingly, Fanta.

The three of them continued, taking turns being knotted up with three knots.

Grizzly Jack
By Nicole Wilder

"May Day! May Day!" I yelled into the speaker. "Oil pressure down! Oil pressure down, Can anyone hear me? Can anyone hear me? I don't know where I am, someone track me. Behind me is Wonder Lake, heading north. Do you hear me? I am heading north."

It was all I could do to keep the plane straight, and keep it in the air. The sky was blue, no wind, all my readings were right, but I was losing oil pressure. I was about to crash. All I could do was try to minimize the damage to myself. A soft landing was all I could hope for.

"God, Please don't let me die. Please don't paralyze me. Please let me live. Please don't hurt me," I said over and over as I tried to keep the aircraft from crashing. I was almost to the ground. If I could just ease it down. Nose in the air. *Please don't crash. Please don't crash.* My mind reeled with thoughts, prayers and regret.

I was in the middle of the Danali National Park in Alaska. No one knew where I was. No one ever comes here. No one lives here, it is all wildlife here. The best I could hope for was to get someone on the radio to find me, land softly and figure out how to make it out of the wilderness alive.

Alive. Alive. Alive. Alive. I was coming in for a landing. Nearly there, thank God there was a clearing to land in.

“MAY DAY! MAY DAY! Please hear me! Please see me! North of Wonder Lake, north of Wonder Lake. Going down! Nearly there... Please, please.”

The plane hit the ground, bounced several times, but stayed upright. It landed hard, but I was okay.

“Stop! Stop!” Please stop.” I said, and then everything went dark.

I felt like I was all there, all in one piece, but where was there? Where was I? Was I dead? I couldn’t open my eyes. I couldn’t remember, what was the last thing that happened? Where was I? What was I doing?

Then I heard nothing.

“Wake up,” I heard someone say, but I still couldn’t open my eyes. The voice wasn’t familiar. It was deep, almost frightening, very gruff, low and impatient.

I’m trying, I tried to say, but couldn’t. There wasn’t any sound coming from my voice at all. It felt like I was in a coma, where was I?

“Come on and wake up,” he said, again. “You are okay, just wake up.”

I tried again to open my eyes. This time I was a success, I opened them. At first everything was blurry, but then I saw shapes, colors and him.

I couldn’t move at first, but as the minutes went on, I could move, feel and talk again.

“Where am I?” I asked the man who stood next to me. He looked huge, as I looked way up at him. He had long brown hair, dark brown eyes, a long brown beard and wore a plaid shirt and jeans.

"You are in Alaska, not far from Wonder Lake, where your plane crashed. You did a great job at landing that thing though. I don't know what happened, but you lost power, and it came down pretty hard. You hit your head, it's going to take you a few days to gain your strength and feel better, and then I will take you into town or wherever you need to go."

He didn't look like he wanted me there, but was going to put up with me, because he had to.

"Am I going to be okay?" I asked, not quite sure what was going on, or what he actually said or where I really was. I was confused beyond anything that I had ever experienced.

"Yes, you will be okay. No broken bones that I can tell, just a bump on the head. I'm guessing it is a slight concussion but that's all." He started to walk away, and that was the last I remembered until what I thought was morning.

"Are you awake?" The man said. I realized I didn't even know his name. I felt much better than the day before.

"Yes, I am. Is it morning?" I asked, still a bit confused. It felt like morning, but I wasn't sure.

"Yes, it is. It is ten o'clock in the morning. Can I get you some breakfast?" He asked, a little less gruff than he had been.

"Yes, please. I'm starving." I hadn't noticed that my stomach was growling until he mentioned breakfast.

Without a word he disappeared down the hall, and I heard pans banging. I got out of bed, and at first the room spun, so I sat back down on the side of the bed. When the room stopped spinning, I tried again. I felt a little woozy, but I could walk. Out of the bedroom and down the hallway, I went in search of the kitchen. When I reached it, I was grateful.

"That smells wonderful," I said, as I entered the room. He had eggs and bacon frying in a skillet.

"Thank you," he said, looking at me. He seemed so much younger now that I could focus. His hair and beard were long, but he was probably only thirty years old, same as me. He was rather handsome under all that hair and gruffness, I even thought I saw him smile.

"Can I take a shower? Would you happen to have anything that I can wear?"

"Yes, and I do."

He left the kitchen and motioned for me to follow him, down the hallway to his bedroom. He went into a box in his closet, fished out sweatpants and a sweatshirt and handed them to me. They would do.

"There are towels in the bathroom." he said.

I stared at him for a moment, feeling his gentleness.

"Thank you."

I turned and went into the bathroom. When I came out, I felt much better, and there was food on the kitchen table waiting for me.

"Thank you," I said again, sitting at the table. "This is a wonderful breakfast."

He sat with me, and began to eat the scrambled eggs.

'What is your name?" I asked him. "Mine is Darcy."

"Jack," he said. "What are you doing up this way?"

"Sightseeing mostly, getting away from things, and I had some supplies to drop off in Denali National Park. Then all that trouble with the plane..."

Having a pilot's license though, was one of the best things that a person could do in the rough terrain of Alaska. It was the best and easiest way to get around.

"I don't think you will be able to repair your plane," Jack said.

I ate slowly. The food tasted wonderful, but just didn't want to go down the way it should. Though I was starving, I still didn't feel so good.

"That sucks. That was my favorite plane," I said. I had two others. The one that crashed was my father's favorite, and now it was mine. My father taught me to fly when I was a teenager. "How will I get out of here?"

"I will take you in a couple of days. I have a radio, and can get a message to someone if you need."

"No, that's okay," I said. I had no one, no one that needed to know. Suddenly I felt pathetic.

"Okay, then enjoy it here." The gruffness was back, and I found I really didn't like him. He really wasn't nice.

"You have a plane?" I asked.

"Yes, I do, so I can take you anywhere."

"Hawaii?" I teased.

He laughed. "I wish."

"You do have a sense of humor," I said, finishing my breakfast.

"At times. I'm sorry. I haven't had visitors in a long time."

"I can tell. Why?" I asked, curiously. Why would someone that young hide himself away?

"I like my life this way. I can do what I want

when I want, and have no one to tell me not to. I love this life."

"So you don't want a girlfriend?"

"No, too much trouble."

With that he got up, went to the living room, and didn't talk to me most of the rest of the day. He kept his distance, though he got me everything I needed.

"I'm going to bed," he said, that evening. "You know where everything is. Help yourself."

He got up and started to go to the bedroom.

"Wait! Did I do something to upset you?" I asked.

"You didn't do anything, I'm just not a people person."

"But you can't be alone forever," I said.

"Yes, I can. Goodnight." Jack walked to his bedroom and forcefully slammed the door.

I felt as though he was continuously angry with me for being there, for being an inconvenience. He could have taken me back to civilization at any time, but he didn't. I knew it was pretty far to town, but if he wanted me gone, then why not?

The house was creepy and lonely, with Jack asleep. I didn't know what to do with myself, so I paced slowly from one end of the house to the other. Soft snoring drifted from his room. He was so quick to fall asleep, while I couldn't stop myself from being antsy. There was something about this man, like a mystery. I almost felt like he had killed someone, and buried them in his backyard. He gave me that kind of a creepy feeling. And yet, at the same, he was kind in his own way. He didn't have to save me, didn't have to take care of me. But he did.

I crept into the blue room that I had occupied, and climbed into the tall, big bed. The white flannel sheets were soft and warm, and the fluffy pillows welcomed my head. I stared at the white ceiling in the dark until all went blank and dreams overtook me.

"Breakfast is ready. I have to go out for a while. You can stay in bed if you want or make yourself at home."

With my eyes only partially opened, I saw Jack's tall, grizzly figure walk out of the room, and heard him leave the house. A few minutes later, a truck engine roared, and then the sound drifted off.

I lay there for the longest time. It was too warm to get out of bed. I am always the warmest and coziest when it's time to get out of bed. I wasn't that hungry, so breakfast didn't seem as important as just lying there. I rolled over and pulled the thick, blue comforter up to my neck and snuggled in.

I jumped up at the sound of a loud bang outside. Before I knew it, I was standing barefoot on the cold floor. I looked at the clock, which said it was 1:00 in the afternoon. The sunshine drifted through the delicate, white curtains that hung in the window. I stumbled out of the bedroom into the living room where Jack stood. He donned blue jeans and a flannel shirt giving off the image of a rugged lumberjack. He stood with his legs parted, his hands on his hips.

"Were you going to sleep all day?" A smile started to cross his face, but then suddenly left again.

"It was just so warm and cozy. Thank you for taking care of me."

"Sure." He turned his gaze to the kitchen, and strolled into it. My eyes focused on his biceps, and for a moment I wondered what his arms would feel like around me. Then my eyesight wandered down to the curve in the back of the jeans and the massive thigh muscles. For one second, I wanted to be trapped within those muscles.

"Wait, don't clean up. I got it. Just let me wake up for a few minutes." I went into the kitchen, and saw scrambled eggs and bacon on a plate on the counter. The pans were in the sink, and Jack started to run hot water to wash them.

"It's okay. I have this." He faced the window behind the sink. "Warm up your breakfast if you want, you must be hungry."

"Yes, thank you." I reluctantly took the plate from the counter, set it in the microwave and pushed a few buttons to start it. Once the buzzer went off, I removed the warm plate, took a fork from the drawer, and sat at the wooden table to eat.

"Do you have everything?" He still wouldn't look at me. What was with this man? Many men told me that I was pretty with my natural, long auburn hair, light blue eyes and slender curves, so I didn't think that it could be my looks.

"I'm fine. Thank you."

I took a tiny bite of the eggs, and realized they needed salt and pepper. As if reading my mind, Jack set the salt and pepper shakers on the table. "Thank you." I used the spices and took another bite, then without bacon.

"I'm going out to do some work in the yard and cut down some trees. If you need anything, you can yell for me." He set the now clean pan into the dish drainer, wiped his hands on his jeans, and walked toward the door.

"Do you need any help with anything?" I took another small bite of bacon, waiting for an answer.

"No, everything is fine. But if you are up to it later, I can take you for a walk around the property." His gaze held mine. There was something tender in his eyes for a split moment, and then it was gone.

"I would like that, if it's not too much trouble. Just let me know when. I'll be ready." He scoffed and walked out the door.

I wished I could figure out what was up with him. He was obviously soft enough to save me, care for me, but he acted like he hated me near him, hated my presence. What was he hiding from me? Why did he treat me the way he did? I didn't know if I wanted to find the answer or just get the hell out of the place.

In the shower, the warm water drizzled down my body and my soapy, long fingers followed it. I thought of a soapy Jack in the shower with the bubbles drifting over his muscles, how it would feel to touch the bulky skin, and what his strong, warm hands would feel like on my own soft curves.

"Stop that," I told myself. I don't know why I thought of those things. He was gruff and almost frightening, and I didn't know how to get through to him anyway.

I finished my shower, toweled dry, and then put on another pair of jeans and blue T-shirt that I found. I had no under clothes, but it was okay.

I looked out the clear windows to see if I could see where he was. Digging a big hole. It was in the shape of a grave plot.

"What the heck is he doing? Is that for me?" Nerves took over causing my pounding heart to make it difficult to breathe. I looked around the house for something I could use for a weapon if I needed it. But instead I found his pictures on the wooden mantle over the dark fireplace. The picture in the gold frame was that of Jack and a woman. They looked very happy. Jack was clean cut and more handsome than I had guessed. The woman smiled and held onto his arm. She wore a wedding dress. I wondered what happened.

"Find something of interest?" His low, annoyed voice sounded behind me. I jumped and my breath was taken away.

"Is this you?" I pointed at the wedding picture.

"Yes." He scuffed to the kitchen, turned the water on, and washed his hands.

"You were married?" I followed him.

"You are really nosey. Yes, I was." He wiped his hands on his jeans again. I wondered if he ever used the towel.

"Divorced?"

"No. Would you like to go for a walk now?" His glare told me I shouldn't ask any more questions, but I felt that I needed to.

"Separated?"

"No, Miss Nosey. My wife was killed in an accident." He looked suddenly sad, broken like an old, neglected toy.

"I'm sorry."

"Do you want to go for a walk or not?" My heart ached for him, and I felt bad for pressing.

"Kind of." The thought of him digging the grave and his deceased wife came to mind.

"Do you or don't you?" His stare scared me.

"To what? The grave you are digging?" I pointed

to the backyard where I saw him digging.

"What?" He hesitated like he didn't know what I meant. "Oh, that? No, silly. I'm using it for compost. A grave?" He started wildly laughing. "I'm not heartless."

"Actually, I was thinking you are."

"I was just hurt. I'm not a killer. Really?" He started laughing again, which caused me to laugh with him.

"I'm sorry, but that's what it looked like."

"Come on, goofy. Let me show you around." He took my hand and for the first time I really saw and felt a soft side to the man.

"What would it take you to say yes to a date, or a flight in my plane?" I looked up at him as we walked through the grass under the bright, blue sky. It was chilly, but not terribly cold.

"You are working on it." He stopped, and I didn't want to push. I let him guide me to all the parts of the yard: The rowboat, the dock, an eagle, a moose, the mountains, and a bear.

"Have you owned this place long?" He still held my hand, and as we walked, I moved every closer to his stocky figure, feeling the warmth and strength. At first he pulled away, then he didn't. It was as if he wanted me close, but wanted me far away. I wanted to know if he would was really gruff, or if I could get through to his soft side that I saw when he smiled.

"It was my grandfather's property. When he died, he gave it to me. He knew I loved this place and the rest of the family isn't partial to it." His gaze held mine again, and I watched the twinkle in his eyes as he talked about his grandfather.

"It's really beautiful." But I didn't take my eyes off him.

"Yes, you are." He looked as shocked to say it as I did to hear it.

He led me back to the house, and when we reached the porch, he stopped, looked down at me. "That was nice. Thank you. It's been a long time since I took a walk with someone."

"I had a nice time, too. Now I will make dinner."

"No, you won't." Jack led me out to the lawn chair on the porch overlooking the pond and mountains. "You just sit here until I call you for dinner. Feel free to take a nap."

"You just want me to shut up for a while," I said. Jack laughed at me, and went inside.

It was so beautiful where I was with the cool breeze, sunshine, pond, eagle flying over, and I could still see the bear. After awhile, I fell asleep to the beauty of it all.

Awhile later I was woken up by, "Wake up, sleepy head. Dinner is done."

When I looked up at Jack, I couldn't believe my eyes. Somehow he managed to cut his hair pretty short and trim his beard close to his face. What a change. What a sexy man!

"Wow! Am I dreaming?"

"Yes, you are," he said, in his gruff tone, and walked away.

I jumped out of the lawn chair. "Wait!" I stopped him by grabbing his arm, and then looked at him again. "I didn't mean to hurt your feelings. You look amazing."

"Thank you." His blue eyes held mine again as if he was trying to figure me out.

"You are beautiful. Your softness reminds me of my wife. She was patient and kind, and never gave up on me. You have that same softness and kindness. I like that about you."

"Thank you. She sounds wonderful."

"She was. I miss her." We stood glued to each other's eyes. "Shall we have dinner?"

"I'd love to." Jack turned and pulled out a chair for me. I smiled up at him, then down at the table. There was two steak dinners with a salad and baked potato. "How wonderful."

"Wine?" He asked, and I turned to see him with the wine bottle.

"Yes, please." Jack seemed so much more open and talkative all through dinner. He was sweet and charming, and deep down I wanted to kiss him. Our walk seemed to show him that it was possible to talk to someone, that it was okay, that I was okay.

"To new friends," I said, holding my glass to his.

"Yes, new friends." His twinkling eyes and bright smile took my breath away.

The rest of meal led to a long conversation about our lives, including his wife.

"Let me do the dishes," I said, when we were finished.

"Let me help you," Jack said. The smile that flashed across his face took my breath away.

"Absolutely," I said, unable to take my eyes off him.

"I'll wash, if you rinse," he said.

"That's a great deal."

I brought all the dirty dishes to Jack to wash. At one point, he dropped a dish into my side of the sink.

Water splashed up and over my shirt.

"Hey, you did that on purpose," I said, teasing him. I took some water and splashed him with it, and laughed.

"I see how you are. I'll get you now." Jack filled a glass full of soapy water and dumped it all over me. He roared in laughter. "You look like a drowned rat!"

"You are so mean," I teased. "Now look at me. I'm soaked."

"And it's a damn good sight, I must say," he said, with a smile.

"Thank you," I said, surprised at the compliment.

Jack handed me a towel. Instead of drying me, I began to dry him off. He stopped me by grabbing me and pulling me close.

"You are a funny girl, Darcy."

"And you like me, even with your gruff exterior," I said. "You can't fool anyone. You are a sweetheart."

"Yes, I do like you, but you might not like my sexual nature," he said, before he brought his mouth down on mine. Though I was surprised, I relished the feeling of being in his arms.

He backed away from me and looked at me like he just regretted what he had done.

"Don't you dare," I said, sensing he was about to tell me how sorry he was for kissing me.

"What?"

"Don't you dare say you are sorry for kissing me, or I will be angry. You know you wanted to kiss me. You know you still want to," I said.

Jack backed away, still looking me. I wondered what he wanted to say.

"But I shouldn't….."

"Before you continue, know that if you do, I will tie you up and take you anyway," I said, semi-teasing.

"Tie me up?" He laughed as if he didn't believe me. I didn't either.

"Yes, I will," I said. "Kiss me again. And again. And again." My voice was muffled by his kisses. My body molded into his, and although I hadn't known him for long, I wanted this. I felt connected.

He picked me up and set me on the table. He reached over into a drawer and pulled out some twine. The evil grin took me by surprise, but I was intrigued. He put my hands behind my back and tied them together. I wrapped my legs around his waist.

Jack began to rub himself against me, almost as if he was making love to me with our clothes on. It was one of the biggest turn-ons I had ever had. I didn't want to hurry, didn't want to rush, and yet, at the same time, I wished our clothes were off.

"Oh, Jack," I murmured between kisses.

In only a moment, his hand was on my wet breast squeezing and teasing through the material. I felt my nipples grow firm at his hot touch. Then he reached for the bottom of my shirt and lifted it up over my head leaving my round, white breasts bare. His lips immediately went to my nipple to lick and nibble. His other hand pleasured my other needy breast. I leaned up against the large wooden table for balance. The aching that I had for him at that moment was all I could think about. I wanted him to take me. I didn't care about being tied up. He could do anything he wanted to me.

He pushed me down and pulled off my pants.

"You want me, don't you?" He asked. "I don't

care. I'm taking you, and since you are tied up, you have no say."

"I don't want one. I'm aching for you. Take me!" He lifted my legs over his shoulders. His head went immediately between my legs. I wrapped my legs around his neck and pulled him closer to me. I felt his tongue on my already hard clit. My body shook as he teased and tasted me. My hips wiggled as he licked me. Then I felt his fingers at my soaked opening. He pushed what felt like several fingers inside me. As he continued to lick me, he moved his fingers in and out of me.

"Oh, Jack, I need to come. Please make me come," I said as I shook all over. The hand that was on his head ran up over my curves until it reached my breast. I squeezed as the pressure of orgasm took over my thoughts, my body. His fingers slipped out of me when he knew that I was coming. The movement of his fingers circling my clit replaced his tongue. I screamed in pleasure at that moment. He continued his assault on my clit for a few moments more before I yelled at him to stop. I couldn't take any more, but there was nothing I could do about it. I was his prisoner.

"I want to please you," I said. "I need to. Please, baby."

He grinned at me, but left my hands tied up. I looked at him with wanting tears in my eyes, but all he did was unzip his pants to leave his hard cock out into his hand. He began to stroke the shaft and leave me to watch. It was so beautiful, so exciting.

"You like it, don't you? You want to touch it, but you can't."

"Yes, yes, I do, but you are so beautiful stroking yourself. It's thrilling."

He stroked faster, touched his balls. Then he brought it to my face, brushed my lips with the head. His hand went to the back of my head, guiding me as he slid in and out. I could feel him watching me suck him. He moaned as his hips thrust forward. He tickled his balls with his fingertips. He squirmed as he continued to let me suck. He pulled away from my mouth, reached behind me and pulled the bow on the twine to set my hands free. Then he pushed me back onto the table.

His cock was so hard that all I wanted to do was feel it inside me. I wrapped my legs around his waist and pulled him near me. "Enter me," and he did as I asked. I shrieked in pleasure as I felt him push into me. He rocked with me there at the kitchen table.

At first his movements were slow and driving me mad with need, and then he began to push into me harder and faster. He played with my breasts as he took me. The pressure of him filling me so deeply and so hard and fast made my body shake in orgasm again.

I was ready for him. I needed to feel his pleasure forcefully enter me.

Jack pushed hard as his body shook and his eyes closed. He held himself very deep in me as he came. The feeling forced my orgasm to continue as we both shook madly against each other.

We stayed that way for a few minutes as we stopped shaking and our breathing slowed again. I didn't let Jack out of me until my mind came back to reality.

We breathlessly put our clothes back on and looked at the mess in the kitchen and laughed.

"It's wonderful being with you. I wish you didn't have to go," Jack said.

"You were trying to kick me out a few minutes ago."

"I was stupid," he said.

"Who am I to disagree?" I said, giggling. "I'm glad you came to your senses. I don't have to go yet. I don't want to leave either. Not yet."

I wanted to stay, to keep getting to know him, keep getting close.

"What if I just keep you?" Jack asked.

"We will see. One day at a time, but I, at least, have to get my clothes and planes from home if I stay," I teased.

I felt so lucky that this all had happened to me. It sucked about losing my plane, and nearly losing my life, but it was great to have this new love in my life.

"For now, I am keeping you then," he said, sweeping me up into his arms and carrying me off to the bedroom. The only thing that we got done that night was each other, but it was a great start to a new chance romance.

Black Lace
By The Vixen

'Oh God'...An arousing sensation shot down her spine. She was exposed, bound and blinded. A thin layer of sweat covered her body, her body glistened under the lights of the illuminated bedroom. Her temperature continued to rise as she awaited his next move. The atmosphere in the room grew more. Her hands were tied with thick black leather handcuffs, attached to the harness on the ceiling. Her desperate breathing was the only thing that broke through the silence.

She was completely helpless.

It was only moments ago he had blindfolded her with a silky black lace embroidered eye mask. The fine silk mask covering her eyes tugged against her skin, as she tried desperately to get a peek through its shielded folds. To no avail. All she saw was darkness. Her hands were cuffed behind her at the small of her back. Time was non-existent. The last thing she had seen was the night sky blanketed with stars out of her bedroom window. She could feel his presence circling around her, she knew he was close. He moved quietly like a predator stalking its prey in the night. She felt his hunger, his desire; everything collided together to create a creature composed by his own need. His breath barely grazed her skin. All her senses were heightened, she was in tune with every sound, scent and vibration in the room. The smell of his fine cologne marked his trail after each step he made. The build-up was exhilarating, the suspense in the air thickened. The soft sensation of his warm lips touched the tip of her ear, as he nibbled it gently. His hot breath tickled her neck. She felt his finger trace her hourglass silhouette, tickling her flesh. God only knows what he had in store for her tonight.

"I have quite the night planned for us," he whispered. He placed his strong hands on her shoulders. She inhaled deeply, as he basked in her sweet jasmine scent. It was her intoxicating soft fragrance that drew him in each time.

He wanted her so badly.

"You will be very pleased," he continued. His hands glided down her curvy hips and made their way towards to her vulva, teasingly grazing her clitoris. She took a sharp breath in as she felt him against her sweet spot. "I want you to always remember this. Tonight I will do things to you that you've only dreamt about." He pressed his face against her hair, inhaling the jasmine there. "You. Are. Mine"

She felt her body pulsate at each word. *You. Are. Mine*...She was his, every part of her belonged to him. There was nowhere else she wanted to be. He was fire, she was ice. He was yin, she was yang. They completed each other, each representing the missing half of themselves they lost and found each time their lips met. They were constantly at battle in a tumultuous love/hate war. No matter how many times they fought, they would come back to one another. They were addicted to each other. Each moment they spent together was more explosive than the next. It was dangerous, but she kept coming back for more.

"Do you belong to me?" he asked. She heard her thunderous heartbeat thumping in her ears.

"Yes," she replied softly, as his fingers slid closer to her pearl, touching it gently.

"Yes what?"

"Yes I belong to you…master." Her voice was meek. Her sight had been taken; her hands were bound together. She was trapped, patiently awaiting his next move. Only he knew how to fulfill her. He rubbed against her sensitive bundle of nerves, until she whimpered. It was the sweet pleasure she had craved so badly. It felt wonderful, she never wanted it to end.

More

That one word echoed in her mind, and drove her crazy. Lost in their lust, she craved him inside of her. Unfortunately she wouldn't get what she wanted so easily. She knew he was going to make her beg for it. He wanted to challenge her in every way until she finally cracked under his seductive assault and gave herself to him completely. As he placed more pressure against her pearl, it took everything in her to hold back her cries. She felt his impatience and arousal grow by the second.

"Are you enjoying yourself?" he asked.

Her body froze.

"Answer me!" His tone had changed, becoming more rigid with his words. His grasp around her shoulder grew tighter. She knew he was not to be trifled with at this moment.

"Are you enjoying yourself?" he muttered before bathing her neck in kisses, standing behind her curvaceous form. She bit back an aching moan, before he could hear it. His hands cupped her hips. She gasped, her body trembling. What did he have up his sleeve? What was he plotting?

His hand traveled upward to her perky breasts. A small moan escaped her lips as he squeezed down her firm bosom. His fingers played with her rosy erect nipples.

"Yes," she whimpered. His lips made a small trail down her neck. Stimulating jolts of pleasure ran through her, as his other hand traveled downward toward her clit. She moaned, and slowly moved her hips against his hand. Both hands simultaneously seducing her. She was moist with excitement, as his fingers dug deeper into her treasure. She was caught in a delirious state of pleasure, as she was at the mercy of his seductive assault on her.

He smirked, she was right where he wanted her.

"You're nice and wet for me," he whispered, taunting her.

She wanted to fight back, but she was bound tightly, and the darkness of her lace eye mask to left her blinded. She felt his breath against her skin.

"If you are trying to make me beg for it, you may want to try a little harder?" A smug grin appeared on her lips.

*How do you like that?...*She was testing him. Another wave of confidence washed over her. She wasn't about to go down without a fight. It was her fiery spirit he was intrigued by. He chuckled and kissed the nape of her neck, placing more pressure down on her sensitive nipples. An erotic moan escaped her plump lips, as his rhythm became more passionate. His grip became tighter, his kisses more desperate. The feeling was exhilarating. Her body was being attacked from every angle. If she wanted to play this game, he would entertain her.

"This is just the tease," he whispered in her ear. "The best has yet to come."

She felt herself getting wetter with each word that rolled off his lips, already regretting her sudden wave of confidence. She knew something sinister was forming in his mind. Her leg started to twitch as her arousal grew, excitement building up in her chest. A euphoric rush of illicit delight surged through the both of them, as his fingers found their way to her clitoris, and rubbed against her sensitive pearl gently. Her moans filled the room getting louder and louder with each passing second. Her thighs shook under his touch, as he inserted another finger into her. His hand was soaked from her horny juices trickling down his hand as they moved in a feverish motion. She almost lost it, Her thoughts were scrambled. All she could do was feel the unfiltered, erotic feeling of pleasure go through her body. It was a torture yet bliss, she couldn't decide which one it was. All she knew was it felt amazing, feeling his erection throb against the curve of her backside. She wanted to feel him inside of her, each pulsating vibration that came from his cock already made her want to come. His lips brushed against her ear.

"You can't come just yet," he teased. She swallowed hard, knowing something sinister was in store. A smirk appeared on her face, she looked forward to it.

He worked his way down her body, until he reached her sweet opening. He planted subtle kisses on her groin, each one made her thigh twitch. She felt his lips get closer to her pearl, her skin now super sensitive to his touch. His hands slowly grasped her plush buttocks and lifted her off the ground so he could take her into his mouth. His tongue moved wildly around her bundle of nerves. She cried loudly, as he moved faster and faster to drive her to the brink of insanity. If she wanted to misbehave, then she would just have to been punished.

"I can do this all night you know," he said moving away from her. He flicked his finger at her clitoris. She shivered. "If you want me in you, you're going to have to tell me what you want. I'm not going to stop unless I hear what I need to hear."

His voice oozed with lust. He tasted her again and as he licked her pearl, she threw her head back in ecstasy. God, it felt amazing, but she wanted to feel more. She bucked up against his tongue in an attempt to feel more of him, but it was no use. He inched away from her purposely, a devilish grin appeared on his face.

"Say it."

She inhaled deeply and lifted her head back.

"Please…" she whimpered. "Please just fuck me…do whatever you want to me."

His smirk widened as he made his way inside of her, sliding his tongue in and out of her moist cavern and sucking up all her sweetness. She bit her lip desperately, holding back her screams. His grasp tightened as he devoured every drop of her essence, and he moved faster. She started to lose it, as his fingers began to slick inside her. He placed her leg over his shoulder to hold her up. She was losing control of her senses, as his tongue played with her clitoris and his fingers explored her warm tightness which was driving her insane. An overwhelming feeling tore through her. The faster he moved, the more delirious she became. She lost herself to his assault. The pleasure was so intoxicating it took her to another place, she felt free. Soft pleasurable sounds escaped from her lips. She felt her barriers falling to wayside.

Just as she was about to lose it, he swiftly moved away from her and removed his hands from her pleasure points. He released her from her restraints. She whined once her tight cuffs were removed. Just as she thought she had her freedom, he swiftly turned her curvy frame around to face him. His lips locked with hers, and they became entangled in a passionate embrace. She envisioned the lustful look in his eyes and his chiseled physique. Each kiss was more explosive than the last. He gripped her thick thighs, and picked her up as he brought them over to the bed they shared together. Her body slowly lowered to the sheets, as he took time to admire her hourglass shape. His body towered over her magnificent body admiring every curve for her heavenly shape. He watched her round breasts raise and fall with each breath she took. Her cheeks were flushed, she was truly a wonderful sight. She was a goddess; a tempting vixen that fed his needs and fulfilled his every single desire.

His sun-kissed complexion glowed, soaking in the seductive ambiance in the room. His finger gently traced the lace embroidery of the black silk eye mask obstructing her vision.

"Before I give you your sight back, I have one more gift for you," he whispered. She felt the devious grin form on his lips. His hand slowly made its way down her elegant form, floating past her breasts and flat stomach all the way down to her wet opening. He grazed the outer lips of her opening which made her moan and her back arch. He took a mental picture of her face in ecstasy, and knew she was ready for what he had in store.

"Well, don't keep me in suspense too long" she said playfully. The back-and-forth game of cat and mouse made their adventures even more satisfying. His touch was addicting; his intoxicating kisses made her delirious. He knelt down facing her wet slit and feasted on her sweet essence. She felt erupting shockwaves throughout her body. His tongue gilded over her sensitive pearl, taking in every part of her. His movements became faster, making her body shake. The feeling of his tongue exploring her innermost cavern was mind-blowing. The illicit feeling of sexual nirvana overtook her, and all she did was crave more. Time became irrelevant, nothing mattered except the explosive sexual high they experienced with each fleeting moment.

He removed his tongue from her clitoris, snaking his way up to her flushed face. He graced her neck with loving kisses, and slowly removed the blindfold from her eyes. Beautiful shades of emerald green flashed in her hypnotic orbs. Those exotic gems glittered in the darkness, smoldering in her lust and her chocolate-brown locks spread across the sheets. She was stunning.

Free from her bounds, she grabbed the back of his

neck, and pulled him into another deep kiss. There was nothing left to hold her back.

"Did anyone ever tell you that you were a big tease, Mr. Campbell?"

He smirked.

"I may have heard that once or twice before, and I usually prefer my woman to leave the formalities at the door."

"I thought you liked people to address you properly," she said jokingly.

"Not the ones I sleep with so that makes you the exception."

"I like the way Mr. Campbell sounds, but I suppose I can settle with just calling you by your first now."

"Marcus isn't the worse name."

"No it isn't," she chuckled.

"Well Silvia is a very beautiful name so I'll stick to that."

"Good," she said as she softly bit his bottom lip.

A pleasurable sigh escaped from him. His alluring goddess rolled them over so that she was on top, straddling him. The view of her bouncy breasts lying on her chest on top of him was priceless. She positioned herself over his erect penis and slowly lowered herself on him. His heart pounded, her tightness was indescribable. He felt her walls squeeze his erection. Once he was fully inside her, she rocked her hips slowly. Their hypnotic rhythm picked up speed as he gripped her sides and pounded against her. Her breasts bounced along with their fast tempo. Her hair flew everywhere as she rode him seductively. He started to slam into her harder, increasing the speed and sending her to new heights. She screamed. Her lustful cries bounced off the walls of the small bedroom.

She felt her climax steadily approaching. His thrusts got desperate, and she could tell he was close. She bounced on top of him riding him triumphantly. She wanted to make him break, a nice payback for all the teasing she had endured. It was time for revenge, and she couldn't think of any better way to repay the favor.

They were lost in a daze, lost in their pleasure. The euphoric climax arrived washing over their bodies that were now connected. They were still for a moment to collect their composure. She rose off his limp member, and fell to the side. They were both exhausted. She lay on her side as her fingers traced small circles on his sculpted chest. The look on his face was priceless, He was lost in the same state of happiness as she was.

"I should tie you up more often," he whispered.

She chuckled.

"I did enjoy myself. Lucky for me I have kinky a boyfriend who loves sex as much as I do!"

"Lucky for me, I have a sex-crazed girlfriend who loves every minute of me teasing her mercilessly!"

She smiled.

"Well I hope you're not tired, because I was hoping to get in one more round..."

"God, I was hoping you say that!"

He leaned in close and gave her a chaste kiss on the lips. She fell into his embrace, and they set the field for another rousing adventure lost.

Femme Soumise
(Submissive Woman)
By V.C.

When the birds chirped outside my bedroom window and the sun hadn't yet come, that meant that it was time for bed, but I didn't want to. I was talking to Dayita online. I sent her a message:

I'm looking forward to our first date tomorrow.

She responded back.

Don't you mean later tonight?

With a smiley emoticon, I wrote:

Yeah.

She wrote back:

I'll admit, I'm kind of nervous. It will either be amazing, or it will suck. I've really liked our conversations. I'm feeling you a lot, like, not in a romantic kind of way, just in that...I really want to be horny with you in person way.

I typed:

Hehehe, I know. I feel that way too.

Her smiley emoticon made me smile. She typed:

No matter what happens, should be fun.

I wrote:

You haven't wasted my time, which is impressive.

Trust me.

She wrote:

You are the real deal.

Quickly, I wrote back with a winking emoticon:

I know. Nannite.

She answered:

Goodnight, Lisa.

After logging off the FetLife instant messenger, it was off to bed for me.

It wasn't common for me to meet women like Dayita online. I was hooked on her since I read (actually *read*) her profile, and viewed her staggering number of pics where she partook in spanking, bondage-play, breath-play, puppy play and pony play. We already shared those common kinks, interests and fetishes. It seemed too good to be true. Dayita was the real deal too. I knew that right away when we first contacted each other. After three weeks of us chatting back and forth, I was going to prove to her that I was the real deal in the flesh, starting with our highly anticipated "date" number one.

***

The night was as sapphire as the blue of my dress. When I entered into the local coffee shop called The Brew Brothers, the grinding of coffee beans in an espresso machine met my ears, and the earthy, chocolaty aroma became the essence of my mouth's desire. And cream. And I wasn't thinking about the kind that would swirl in my coffee.

Sitting at a table that was far enough from the entrance but near enough to where Dayita could see me when she'd walk in, I looked at my watch. I had told her to meet me at 8:00 on the dot. Not a second less or later. It was 7:59 P.M. My lips curled with satisfactory delight, when Dayita arrived precisely at eight on the dot just as I expected from her.

Good, I thought. *She looks to be a very promising sub already.*

When my eyes first glanced at her from my seat, I couldn't help but slide my tongue over my lips and smudge my cherry-red lipstick in the process. And not giving a flying fuck to re-apply it again for first appearances sake. Dayita was worth the minor imperfection. Seeing her in pics where she was gagged, tied up or being spanked was always a pleasure, but in the flesh, I mouthed,

"Wow."

She was looked as sexy and alluring, in her tight-fitting black jeans, red buttoned-up blouse and leather jacket, as she did in her leather pony play gear, bottom-less vinyl mini skirt, and leather O-ring embellished corset. Dayita was so tame and demure in person, it made her darker, kinkier side—the one that I knew all too well already—even more incredibly hot. That's because I knew better. She was a freaky deaky woman like me.

When she approached me, I stayed in my seat, looking at her.

"Hi, Lisa. Nice to meet you!" she spoke chirpily with a smooth and seductive Indian accent, and flashed her bright white megawatt smile at me.

"You arrived just on time. Good girl."

And boy, wasn't she ever. She was *extremely* good-looking, she truly was an Indian beauty: curvy and full-figured and dark-skinned as well, as dark as the coffee we were about to drink at any moment now. It was going to be extremely hard for me to not think about drinking her as we sat down to drink our hot, oh so hot, cup of coffee together. *Later, Lisa. Much, much later.*

Other than her luscious curves, her phenomenal big bottom, and her round-as-melons pair of breasts, the most striking feature of all that I admired the most in her pictures, but admired all the more in the flesh, was her hair. She had the thickest, shiniest raven hair I had ever seen. Not only was it thick and shiny, but it was *long*. Her luminous black locks hung well past her bottom, touching the back of her knees. She had it tied in a ponytail, and her hair even passed her knees. It was incredible, it had to be seen in the flesh to truly believe that it was real. Just like she was. Completely real. Too real to be true. Not that I didn't know that from ogling over her profile pictures, but to see her hair before my eyes, to see how long it was in person, was quite a sight. Just like her face. I don't know what it is about Indian woman, but their features always brought out a—I will not say *exotic*, how cliché would that be!—rather stupendous majesty that even made a top like me want to stand on my knees, bowing at their majestic comeliness.

And I *love* dark-skinned women. I've always cherished how my paler apricot skin creates such a gorgeous ebony and ivory contrast, especially when we were breast-to-breast, crotch-to-crotch, hand-in-hand or hand-to-bottom. Her eyes were as dark as that of a raven's feathers too: ethereal, enchanting and eerie. It was in those ink-black eyes of hers that I saw a rumbling heat that did more than make me hot, it scalded me. If that wasn't a sign that we had an instant connection, I didn't know what else would be.

"What kind of coffee would you like, Madame?" she asked me coyly.

"Espresso. Double shot. One pack of brown sugar."

"Yes, Madame." she nodded.

"I love the way you say Madame," I cooed.

"Why's that, Madame?"

"Just get my coffee."

She obeyed me, and ordered our beverages. When she returned to our table, and set my beverage before me. I took a sip of the espresso, eyeing her intensely. She sat there, her nervousness so soft and subtle in her face and eyes. I could practically sense that she was crossing her fingers, if not from under the table, definitely in her mind.

"It's perfect." I smiled at her after taking another sip of the espresso.

"Oh, thank God." She chuckled, as did I.

There was not once a dead moment of awkward silence. Our conversation was nothing but similarities, common likes and interests. Especially when it pertained to the most glorious subject of all: the erotic. Once we got to that topic, we couldn't stop. We talked about what really turned us on. What made us as horny as two bitches in heat. What made us so wet that it could make the Sahara desert run with water for the first time. What made us crave, moan, cry, beg, plead and come for our lives. What made us want nothing else more but that one kinky and erotic thing that made us feel crazy this way. Something so great that we couldn't possibly live a day without it.

"What is your greatest escape, the kind that you can't live without?" I asked her with my husky southern Texan drawl, sipping my last drop of espresso.

"For me, it's got to be bondage…" She licked a droplet of her chai tea latte from her thick and luscious dark lips, savoring the last drop from the corner of those gorgeous beauties.

I wished I could have licked it off for her, but she did it before I tried.

Tease.

"Why is that?"

"Bondage tops all!" she declared.

"Oh yes, it sure can!" I beamed.

"It's kinda funny. I wouldn't say I'm the most submissive person in the world. I'm actually quite picky as to who I submit to, but when I do, when my dom or mistress ties me up... I become totally his or hers in mind, body and soul. I know that sounds quite extreme but—"

"It's not extreme at all." I purred. "It's fucking hot and stimulating, that's what it is."

"I noticed in your profile pictures on FetLife that you are into bondage as much as I am…"

"It's one of my favorite kinky hobbies."

"I *loved* the pics on your profile where you have your partners tied up in places that I could never imagine being tied up at. Beyond just dungeons and the kink party settings, I mean. Like how you have them strapped to trees, tied up in a swimming pool, bound against street sign poles…" She shook her head in disbelief. "How do you get away with it?"

"I just do. I'm good at what I do," I bragged. "And what can I say? I enjoy taking a walk on the wild side when it comes to bondage play. Sure, I do have fun doing it behind closed doors, but performing bondage in public is far more exciting to me. I love the danger and thrill of it."

"It does sound dangerous and thrilling! Looks that way too. I've always wanted a dom or mistress to be as adventurous as you, but they were always too chicken shit to take it that far…"

"You've always wanted to be tied up in public?"

"Yes…" She bit her lip naughtily. "It's been one of my most desired fantasies, but it hasn't come true yet."

"What a pity." I pouted. "Sounds like you haven't found the right partner yet."

"*Yet…*" She emphasized the word, hinting by with a glimmer of lust and desire in her eye that she wanted that partner to be…*me.* "Lisa," she cooed my name. "You are such a total boss."

"Boss is my middle name sweetheart." I winked at her. "You know what I'm attracted to the most about you Dayita, other than your intelligent mind and infectious personality?"

"What's that?" She rested her chin on her duckbill shaped hand. It not only suggested that she wanted to know more about me, but that she must have a private affinity for fisting too.

"Your hair."

"My hair?" She fluttered her eyelashes teasingly, caressing her hair. "It's so *long*!"

So much so that she couldn't possibly get her fingers through it, from scalp to tips in its ponytail form.

"I love it! It must have taken your whole lifetime to grow it that long."

"Just about." She smirked. "I've only had a haircut maybe once or twice in my life, when I was a little girl living in Mumbai. Since I moved to America, I haven't had it cut once."

"Very impressive, my dear. I bet people have had a lot of fun with it…"

"That's an understatement too!" She giggled. "More fun than I dare to say or think about..."

"Your hair must be as kinky as it looks too."

"Kinky?" She let out a loud laugh, sounding a bit surprised. "How is my hair kinky?"

"I will show you soon enough, my sweet…"

I grabbed the end of her ponytail, pulling her towards me, pressed my lips against hers and slipped my tongue into her warm mouth. Her breath smelled like cinnamon and cloves from her chai tea latte. That spice did not only come from the chai tea latte, but from our genuine feverish connection. It made me ever so much more thirsty and hungry, for her amazing mouth. My tongue probed her mouth as its own, and her tongue probed mine driven by that same fever. A fever that wouldn't stop burning. The harder our tongues probed, the harder we moaned and the more that we sizzled.

"Shit…" She gasped when I sucked her bottom lip, giving it a strong commanding pull before letting it go and setting it free from my teeth. "You're a *phenomenal* kisser, Lisa…"

"So are you, Dayita…" I had to catch my breath a little. "That was a phenomenal kiss indeed…"

She leaned in, demanding more kisses and

expected me to obey. I gave her a playful smack to her cheek that made her gasp as if she just had an orgasm. For all I knew, maybe she did.

"Nuh-uh," I wagged my finger at her, shaking my head in disapproval. "Don't be greedy. There is a lot more from where that came from…" I cooed. "Ready to go to the movie?"

"Yes!" she gasped loudly as if I was asking her… *are you ready for me to fuck you?*

That would come soon enough too. Later. Maybe tonight, if Dayita was a very good girl.

"Alright then." I rose from my seat, holding my purse. "Let's go."

The movie theatre was only a block away from the coffee shop, literally right around the corner from it. It was not the typical mainstream Cineplex, it was an arthouse movie theater that showed mostly indie films. Even the indie films that they showed there were far from the normal indie films that you would see in most art-house theaters. The movies ranged from contemporary, science fiction, westerns and steam punk. Tonight, Dayita and I were going to see a contemporary indie film that was far from ordinary. It was—based on what I heard from word of mouth, and read in a couple of arthouse magazines—rated R. Rated R was being light and coy. It would be rated XXX, if it weren't for it being an "artsy" film by an even artsier director who was only getting started.

The film was called *Les Aventures d'une Femme Soumise.* The title alone--*The Adventures of a Submissive Woman*—was suggestively erotic enough. Not only was it an erotic artsy film, but it was also a contemporary one mixed with surrealism. Quite a kooky combination, and an even kookier choice of film to choose for a first date. It wasn't as if this was a surprise. Dayita knew exactly what type of movie we were going to see for our first date.

"I can't wait to see this," she said to me while we were in the queue.

"Me too. I have high hopes for this."

"Oh, I have a feeling that we won't be disappointed at all. The reviews for it have been amazing. One I read said that…" She paused for a moment. "It said that it's sex without touching."

"Trust me. There will be plenty of touching between you and me."

She grinned.

"Oh?"

"You're so goddamn cute, how do you act so innocent."

"I try…"

"You don't try, you just do. Turns me on."

"You turn me on, this must be fate."

"Fuck fate." I stared at her intensely, and her submission was immediate. "I'm in control of this date."

"Yes, Madame."

And my control of the date, and *her*, started when…

Thirty minutes into the film, the female lead, the *femme soumise*—a naïve but gorgeous woman named Colette, whose innocent baby-doll face could very well have her pass off as jailbait if it weren't for the fact that she was actually of legal age, just very young-looking—is in a BDSM dungeon-meets-stripper-club atmosphere. She is pinned helplessly against a stripper pole by a tall and leggy, long auburn haired, blue-eyed, curvy-figured babe with the finest ass and the most phenomenal tits that has ever graced a movie screen. To make the scene even better, she wore a scantily clad outfit that left very little to the imagination. This scene in particular was the most talked about, because the actress playing the role of the dominatrix was a trans-woman. And fuck, what a smoking hot trans-woman she was! She was in total control of the *femme soumise*; the latter was the puppet and she as her dominatrix was her puppeteer. Anything she wanted her to do, Colette did it without needing to raise her voice or lift a finger to tell her what to do. The *femme soumise* was no longer human ,she was her mistress's prop for an audience of what looked to be at least forty men and women.

Not only would the mistress to show off her pet, but show off just how much of a bad-ass mistress she could be. She proudly wielded a shiny pair of handcuffs; they glimmered by the beaming stage lights that were showered upon them like rain. She slapped them on the *femme soumise*'s wrists faster than my eyes that blinked, that quickly. I was truly in awe of the performance, by just that moment alone. I was all the more immersed by Dayita who was as immersed by the movie, if not more, than I was. With her mouth slightly open in wonderment, she couldn't keep her eyes off of that wicked mistress as she then wielded a whip. But in her hand wasn't a whip, it was her ten-inch long penis.

"Oh shit…" I heard Dayita's sharp gasp, as sudden as the sound of thunder and eyed her with a smile as mischievous as the audience in the movie who watched the ten-inch cock wielding mistress whip the *femme soumise's* ass with her appendage. The cock-whipping was so incredibly loud and strong—and oh so wonderfully real!—that you could actually *hear* her cock slap against the *femme soumise's* flesh. It wasn't a sound effect either. The budding red cock-head imprints against her pale-skinned buttocks were indeed very real, not an illusion brought on by special effects makeup. I had to catch my breath, I was more than turned-on. I was deeply moved. Most people would consider this to be total porn, glorified porn, but in reality, it was far from being cheap, dirty and mundane like everyday porn. It was all in the execution, the slick, gorgeous and stylistic way that it was filmed. The attention to detail on the mistress's face, the way her eyes expressed such dominance and control, fearlessness and restlessness. And on the *femme soumise's* face, the way her facial expressions displayed all sorts of emotion: pleasure, pain, fear and most of all, love. Love from the thrill of being a *femme soumise* for an audience of fellow perverts and freaks to fawn, gawk at and admire as a piece of sex-meat.

This was not only a showcase of impeccable filmmaking, but truly a piece of art.

"Are you enjoying this?" I whispered into Dayita's ear, licking her earlobe.

"Yes…" She quivered when I sucked her ear a little.

Oh yeah. She was already my…sex-meat.

"What do you like the most about what you're seeing?"

"The mistress's cock…" She gulped. "The way she's using it to whip her submissive…"

"And what else…"

"How the submissive is all tied up…"

"That's right. You really like that, don't you?" I caressed her neck with the tip of my finger, making her flesh quiver too. "To be all tied up…" I grabbed her ponytail, giving it a jerk and pull, making her gasp loudly enough for a few people in the theatre to look towards us only to look away quickly. I whispered into Dayita's ear. "You want to be tied up right now while watching that mistress whip the shit out of that little subby with her monster cock?"

"Here?" She looked at me with eyes that screamed *are you serious?* "Right now, really?"

I tugged at her pony tail harder, making her gasp softly again.

"Put your hands behind your back…" I whispered snappily into her ear, stroking it one more time with the tip of my wiggling tongue.

"Yes ma'am…" she mouthed, doing exactly as she was told.

Gripping the end of her ponytail tightly, I guided it towards her wrists that were already bound against each other, pressed firmly together and behind her back *sans* bondage. I wrapped the length of her long tresses around her wrists, wrapping tighter and tighter until her hair transformed into a thick cuff. It amazed me just how thick and sturdy her hair was, *perfect* for bondage play. Instead of a lock and key to hold the bondage together, I sealed her bondage by tying the rest of her hair into a knot so tight that there was no way in hell that she could escape from it. She couldn't escape even if she were Houdini. She intentionally squirmed and writhed for me with all her strength and might, showing off my work of bondage art and to also prove that she was indeed bound and tied up to the point where she could hardly move anything more than her fingers. Even in the darkness of the movie theater, the light from the movie screen made it abundantly, wonderfully clear that she was *my* femme soumise and I was her mistress. Her mistress without a ten-inch dick. If I did have one, I'd do precisely what the mistress was doing to the *femme soumise* at that moment when I had Dayita literally tied up with her Rapunzel-like hair.

She exposed her penis for everyone in the audience to see, standing proudly and statuesque. She faced the audience, shimmying her phenomenal breasts and wiggling her hips so her cock, too, would jiggle to the beat of her own sexual deviance. Then, she faced her *femme soumise* again. This time, instead of using her cock as the whip to smother her buttocks with red blotches, she used her *femme soumise* to serve her royal monster majesty. Again, the director's artistic styling of the scene that was about to take place was one that should be documented and immortalized in the film history books. The mistress literally jumped on the pole, hanging above her *femme soumise* upside down, while twirling around it with the grace of a ballerina. She was twirling and posing at the same time on the stripper pole, in sync with the trip-hop music that blended in with the hypnotic and seductive mood. She even stretched her leg out as if she was a ballerina—perhaps she was, in real-life—*en pointe*, twirling around the pole one last time above her submissive's head. The *femme soumise* looked up at her, in disbelief by her stylized pole-dancing. How she made it look so easy. That look of disbelief, shock and awe was eerily reflective of Dayita's facial expression when I spread her legs wide open, pulled down the zipper of her pants and pulled her pants down enough to expose her underwear. She wore silky red panties, as shiny and luminous as her raven-black hair.

"You are so very wet..." I whispered into her ear, as I lightly fondled my fingers against her crotch, feeling her nectar seep past the silky fabric. "Bondage makes you this horny, huh?"

"Yes it does..." She quivered. "But it's not just the bondage. And it's not just this movie..."

"What else is it?"

"It's...*you.*"

Her panties were pulled to the side immediately after she said *you*, my lips trembled the instant my fingers rubbed against her pussy. Her slit was so hot, I could smell her heat. It smelled so divine! I rubbed my two fingers against it; it felt as soft as silk, so gooey with her nectar that was overflowing from the horny depths of her. We both kept our eyes glued to the movie screen as the mistress, still on the pole except this time with her crotch facing her submissive's mouth, commanded her to open her mouth. She obeyed just as Dayita obeyed me when I told her,

"I don't want you to make a sound as I finger-fuck you silly..."

She bit her lip and nodded quickly, squirming in her bondage, seeming in both pain and pleasure by her hair captivity. Not that it distracted her; it was the sight of the mistress impaling her submissive's mouth with that monster cock of hers. She did it so swiftly, her cock hammered into her submissive's mouth like that of a beast in heat. In a mere minute, the mistress looked about ready to explode, as evident from the close-up shot of her eyes rolling to the back of her head as she continued to throat-fuck her poor *femme soumise.* As she did it, she gyrated her hips side to side to the music that continued playing. It was hypnotic and entrancing. More than that, it was unbelievable! I couldn't keep my eyes off the screen…

"Shh…" I covered Dayita's mouth a little when she made a loud sound of pleasure.

I pulled her panties further to the side, sliding three fingers inside of her wet, hot, slippery and silky-textured snatch. I pumped them in and out of her in the same motion, as the mistress pumped her cock fast and furiously down her submissive's throat. Oh hell, if I had a dick, I'd sure as hell be fucking Dayita's throat just like that. Right here, right now, in this movie theatre for the ten people in the theater to watch live. Alas, what a pity that I didn't, but my fingers worked just as well. Dayita was practically in tears, writhing in her bondage and biting on her lip hard to prevent herself from moaning or screaming, as I hammered my fingers into her harder and deeper.

I found it unbelievable that Dayita's facial expressions of lust, desire and disbelief mirrored that of the *femme soumise*. The camera focused in on the *femme soumise*, her expressions seemed to intentionally mimic Dayita's. My eyes were a camera lens, focused on Dayita. She opened her mouth but nothing came out, her lust-sounds muted. Despite her silence, I heard her crying and wailing my name, begging me to fuck her harder and deeper so she could scream and shout, if only in her mind. There was going to be no screaming or shouting going on, but I could hear it and feel it, her upcoming release, that inevitable box office hit. I imagined it being just as loud as the screaming and the shouting of the *femme soumise.* Her mistress cock-hammered into her throat harder and harder. The mistress and I were in sync with each other, I pounded into Dayita with the same hard and heavy, hot and horny, fast and furious rhythm as she was her submissive with her cock. She pumped in and out of her submissive's mouth faster…harder…faster…and then…she let out a toe-curling cry of ecstasy, signifying that she was…

"I'm coming!" Dayita whispered loud enough for only me to hear. "Oh yeah, yeah, I'm coming!"

There it was: that amazing gushing of pussy juice. My favorite hot beverage of all time that even takes the cake for coffee, my secondary obsession and craving. There was so much for me to drink.

"You *are* a good girl." I paddled my fingers inside of her, making her pussy make the sweetest clicking sounds from her post-arousal. "You were so nice and quiet, not making a sound…"

I slipped my fingers out of her and sucked her juices off of my fingers.

"It was not easy," she whispered low. "Especially while watching this…I don't ever want this movie to end! It's so fucking good…"

"You're just saying that because you didn't want me finger-fucking you to end while we are watching this!" I laughed lightly, so as to not disturb the audience from the movie. "You liked it."

"You know me already…" her big dark eyes looked into my bright blue eyes as she murmured,

"Except for one thing. I didn't like what you did to me. I *loved* what you were doing to me…"

I slowly and carefully unraveled the knot from Dayita's hair and whispered into her ear, "*Moi aussi, ma femme soumise…*"

For Her Own Good

By Salome Wilde

"And how was the horrid Count?" queried Ania, her nose scrunched in distaste within her slender, doe-eyed face. She had obviously been asleep on Nati's pallet, waiting for her return. Ania perked up as soon as the lovely older woman she thought of as a combination guardian, confidant and servant returned. "Bet he was as ugly as an old horse," she added with a sleepy, girlish giggle.

"Hush," answered Nati, shaking her head. She was tired from the rough treatment the foreign nobleman had given her, and now bore news she relished as little as his touch. The man was more comely than Ania might credit, but he had no interest in his partner's pleasure and more than a slight sadistic streak. As she went to pour herself a small glass of wine to ease her throat and her mind, Nati could only hope she had worn the beastly aristocrat out sufficiently to make him tamer the next night. She wished at least that much for sweet, spoiled Ania, for there was little more she could provide now.

Throughout the harem—perhaps throughout the castle, the story of Ania was common knowledge.

Formerly a lady at the court of her home city, Ania had been a pampered child who'd grown into a willowy, doe-eyed young woman. To Nati, who'd fallen from an even higher estate as a bastard of the King's younger brother, Ania was an overindulged, vain creature who did all she could to deny the reality in which she was living. Even so, she clung to Nati as a sort of mother figure, and Nati was not immune to her charms. Ania was soft-spoken, lovely as a nymph, and she indulged Nati by listening to her read from the books of poetry she loved so well. On nights when Nati was not needed in the chambers of one or another noblemen or women—or occasionally his majesty himself—Ania would cuddle up beside the older woman on her large, soft pallet, and wait for Nati's smooth, rich voice to lull her to sleep with the words she read with devotion. Nati would stroke her golden hair, enjoying the small warmth of her pale body and the two would sleep, entwined. Too grown to be her child, too naïve to be her sister, and far too innocent to be her lover, Ania was unique in Nati's life and knew she was unique in Ania's as well.

Because of this, and with the limited privilege that was Nati's by birth and no little skill at the art of intimacy, she'd been able to coax the King into a modicum of patience with the former Lady Ania. After all, while Nati had known from youth that harem life was the best she could expect from the jealous and autocratic King, Ania had had her fine life ripped from her delicate grasp with abrupt ferocity. Her future hopes and dreams—however superficial they might have seemed to the worldly Nati—had been unjustly stolen from her when it was discovered upon her mother's deathbed that Ania was not her father's daughter after all. She was the fruit of a tryst between her mother and a handsome performer with a traveling actors' troupe. His wife barely cold in the ground, the man who had cradled this precious child from the earliest moments of her life and who would soon have selected a husband for her now that she was of age had unceremoniously dispatched her as "tribute" to the King. He could not bear to look at her now, he reasoned, so why not gain favor by letting the monarch make good use of her?

Even with her ability to live in a childlike state of denial, surely Ania must know that this is exactly what would soon happen. She was, Nati knew, a virgin, and one of astonishing ingenuousness over matters of the flesh. She had been taught to wash and dress herself, as well as to serve herself at the common table. There were few actual duties for the young "princess," as several of the others of the harem called her, and this sadly reinforced her sense of entitlement. She saw Nati as her protector, but did not credit her with the delay of her inevitable sexual service. All Nati's efforts to educate the child-woman on matters that would soon be vital—from managing her monthly blood to methods of preventing conception—fell on deaf ears. Ania did listen and obey, but she refused to acknowledge the purpose behind the advice. At last, however, the moment came when Nati knew she must somehow make Ania understand. Frustrating as the brat might be at times, Nati would prefer her first sexual experience not be traumatic. While, in terms of kingdom law, a harem member could not be raped, she could be in body.

Nati finished her wine in a few gulps, knowing water would have soothed her parched throat more effectively and slipped beneath the furs. She leaned back on ample pillows as Ania neatly laid her head on Nati's lap and curled around her thighs. Nati smiled indulgently holding her close, pleased she'd washed away the Count's seed and a few small traces of blood before returning to her quarters. As they lay together, Nati wondered if this might be the last moment they'd share with such easy comfort. So much would change for Ania the next night, the Count might not even let her return before dawn.

Pushing those thoughts momentarily from her mind, Nati looked around the large, open chamber. Though it was late, not all in the harem quarters were asleep. Nati sighed deeply as she marked the contrast between the pasty young noble she had just left and Rau. Rau, a swarthy giant sat before her, incongruously, on silken pillows playing chess. He always played with Cellet, a foreign-born coquette who boasted a combination of exotic genitalia and the most horridly crooked teeth a human being had ever been given. Cellet smiled a greeting at her, and Rau turned and grunted. Nati blew him a kiss. She knew he was concentrating, determined to beat his opponent as always. Neither of the pair was particularly adept at chess, but they were pleased with each other's quiet company.

The variety in the sex slaves was an endless source of fascination to the kingdom's visitors: from a blushing young maiden from the North with hair that touched the floor who spilled copious tears at every opportunity to the dark, angular crone Ninsi Ra-Ninsi

Ama-Ninsi (Ninsi daughter of Ninsi daughter of Ninsi), whose tattooed tongue was the stuff of legend. The men were equally splendid and diverse, if fewer in number, from two men known only as The Twins—lithe, androgynous youths who could twist themselves into any position required—to Rau, the great, muscled beast of a man who could twist interested lords and ladies in similar fashion.

"Tell me," Ania prodded, and with a gentle nuzzle to her hip, returned Nati's attention to the matter and individual at hand.

Nati considered sharing the details, from his use of random insertable objects as "foreplay" to his lackluster fuck, accompanied by vicious hair- and nipple-pulling. The only thing that had stopped the brute from lashing her with the whip he bound her wrists with was the King's prohibition on marking his playthings. One needed special permission for that, and he had not obtained it. What he had obtained—exactly how Nati did not know—was permission to claim the harem's eldest virgin, Ania. The thought sickened her, as she pulled the furs up over Ania's shoulder.

"Go to sleep. We'll talk in the morning."

She reached for a book beside the pallet, wondering if she could even read.

Ania's response had the opposite of the intended effect. She popped up, pushed the book away, and scowled into Nati's face.

"You enjoyed it!" she accused.

At any other time, Nati would have laughed. Ania's obvious jealousy was so inappropriate and foolish on so many levels.

"I did not," she said, meaning it.

Ania seemed pleased by her answer.

"Well," she said with a pout, "you could have, though."

This was an accusation, and not unfamiliar territory. Ania disparaged Nati's ability to wrest pleasure from even the most distasteful of scenarios. It was a skill she had learned from Rau, and was possessed by many of the harem as a worthy strategy. By contrast, Ania's answer to all questions of what she knew about sex, and what she envisioned for her own future seemed to come straight from the most honeyed of fairy tales.

"A handsome prince," Ania would say, "will rescue me and show me what love is."

She said this often, and all who heard her proclamation would laugh heartily, assuming she was playing coy and making a joke. Only Nati seemed to understand that this "princess" was in earnest.

Tonight, however, there could be no laughter. Nati knew that Ania's destined "prince," would do anything but rescue her. She felt helpless. Yet, as Ania flung her ignorant barb, Nati recognized a new possibility. She knew the best way to get Ania to blossom into the sexual maturity she would need for survival was to learn to pleasure herself, to use her own hands to explore and exploit the unique flower of her sex. Nati had told Ania so, but she would not hear of it.

"It is one thing," she explained, with characteristic naïve boldness. "to be forced to accept lustful advances. But it is worse yet to seek ways to become even more shameless." Occasionally, the scene went differently: Ania would simply deny that Nati meant what she suggested and she'd return to fantasies of her glorious escape in the arms of her handsome, presumably asexual, hero.

"Rau," Nati called suddenly. "Come and help me with this impossible princess."

Ania whimpered her distress. Rau rose and Cellet, chuckling, joined him. Several others who were lying on their pallets but still awake came along as well: including a short, rotund woman whose name Nati did not know as she did not seem to speak the language and the sleepy-eyed voyeur Ingh, who stretched as he walked to witness whatever apparent action was going to take place. Ingh's cock, enormous when flaccid and unthinkable when hard, made him a popular choice for anal punishments given to members of court who displeased the King. He was otherwise unremarkable but for his attraction to Sujuru, a woman whose hair was as wild as her temper and who remained snoring in his pallet when he left.

Though she regretted calling Rau for the attention it brought, she would not relinquish this opportunity, the last she might have to assist Ania in accepting her fate.

"If you let him spank me..." Ania protested, pointing at a smiling Rau.

Nati took Ania's hand and smiled genuinely.

"Nothing of the sort, dear one. Our friends are going to help you achieve something important tonight."

Rau cocked his head, Cellet giggled with nervous arousal and the little fat cherub of a woman quirked an intrigued eyebrow. Ingh remained expressionless, and folded his legs beneath him. The Twins sat too, and the others followed suit.

Nati adjusted herself so Ania sat between her legs, facing away. Ania fidgeted but let herself be maneuvered, likely because she enjoyed the attention and trusted Nati completely. Perhaps too much.

"Because she cannot do so herself, we are going to give Ania a gift."

She looked down at Ania's upside-down face, which frowned in puzzlement.

"A gift?" whimpered Ania, frozen by confusion.

Deftly slipping from beneath her and pinning Ania's wrists overhead, she had Rau remove the furs and firmly yet gently spread and hold her ankles. Ania panicked and bucked. The Twins came each to either side of her, and carefully held down her hips while Cellet sat beside Ania's distressed face, and stroked her cheek softly.

"Easy now," cooed Cellet with a crooked smile. "No one is going to hurt you." She sounded as if she were taming a wild horse. When Ania began to cry, Cellet dabbed the corners of her eyes with the edge of her short robe.

Nati summoned the woman whose name she did not know, and asked her to take Nati's place. The woman understood, and grinned widely. This freed Nati to retrieve several gauze scarves from the nook where her garments hung. When Ania wailed her name with pitiful desperation, Nati hurried back and set to work.

Carefully but firmly, Nati bound Ania's wrists together, bent her arms at the elbows and let her headrest to keep them in place. The grinning cherub leaned back to watch, still ready to stop any attempt Ania might make to escape. Nati looped silk beneath each of Ania's knees, pressed them back, and had The Twins grasp one each at shoulder height. With nimble fingers, she raised Ania's gown to expose her flaxen mound and small breasts. The pink of her nipples matched that of her folds, and all murmured delight in her youthful beauty. Only Ania herself did not know how lovely she looked, bound neatly, open wide to whatever Nati might wish to do to her…for her. She cried loudly, stilling only when Nati spoke again.

Settling herself between the girl's slender thighs, she looked into her moist eyes.

"Don't be afraid, precious Ania. As you said, 'It is one thing to be forced.' We, your friends, will "force" you this one time, and I promise you shall thank us ever after."

Ania ceased struggling, and sobbed.

She knows now that she must be one of us, thought Nati. *And soon she will be*. She reached for a vial of scented oil beside her pallet, and slickened her fingers. Rubbing her hands together to ensure they were adequately warm, she brought both down to smooth along Ania's pubic mound and then around to the backs of her thighs and ass. Ania gasped and stiffened, biting her lip hard. Ingh, who had been passively watching from a distance while stroking himself, leaned in and, taking the vial, drizzled oil lightly over Ania's belly and pubis. Again, Nati smoothed her hands over Ania's delightfully soft, firm flesh, caressing first her breasts and then the flesh beneath her glistening curls. She reached under the girl, to knead the tension from her hips.

Sensual massage soon took at least some of the tension from her body, but when one of The Twins let his grip slacken, Ania began to cry and flail again. Rau let out a single bark of laughter as the blushing Twin pulled her leg back sharply.

"Clearly," said Rau to Nati with a wink, "this one can only consent to a non-consensual experience."

Cellet shushed him, attempting, it seemed, to bring some solemnity to this ritual, and then went back to dabbing the girl's overflowing eyes with great tenderness.

Knowing Ania would not give in until she saw some reason to, Nati parted her labia and oiled her well. Stroking her inner lips softly until she rested a fingertip on her tiny clitoris with great delicacy, she delighted in making Ania jump. The Twins held her, bound and still, and the pleasuring continued. Nati rubbed the hood of her clit in tiny circles, then reversed direction. Simultaneously, she separated two fingers of her other hand into a V, and rubbed between the two deep pink sets of lips. She teased Ania's tiny bud into a blossom, and Ania's breath left her in a moan. Leaning over her body, Nati kissed her mouth softly.

"Now," she whispered, "since you will not do so for yourself, let me show you some true magic."

She crouched between Ania's spread thighs and bent her head forward, offering her mouth in worship. Her fingers still formed a V and stroked the slick flesh. Nati stretched Ania's vulva wide, and placed her wide wet tongue there. Lapping avidly yet gently, she brought the little nub even more fully to attention and felt the labia swell around it. As Ania's hips began to rise, Nati met them by clamping her mouth softly around her clit and began to suck. As she did, she slipped her two fingers deftly down Ania's lips and then inside her. Scented oil and Ania's juices mixed into a sweet and heady fragrance that Nati inhaled hungrily. She stroked inside and up, searching for a little rough patch of flesh that would bring even greater waves of pleasure to Ania.

Ania bucked and writhed under Nati's expert touch and relentless mouth. Reaching a hand up to toy with a nipple, Nati found other fingers already there—no doubt Cellet's. She took the other nipple between her forefinger and thumb and began a gentle, rhythmic tugging. Listening as she sucked, stroked, and pinched, she heard the heavy breathing of her assistants and the rhythmic milking of an oiled cock. Over it all were the soft, low groans of Rau. Nati felt herself grow moist and hot at the delight of it all. She carefully hiked her hips. The pleasure of the climax Ania was sure to experience any moment, spread to the Rau. Nati fought to retain her concentration and coordination as she felt his massive hands grasp her hips, and then his thick, hard cock stretch her wide as he pressed inside.

Nati moaned deep in her throat as she was spread and plundered, resting on an elbow as she quickened her fingers' pace on Ania's swollen insides, her tongue on her clit and she sucked with increasing force. When Ania began to murmur "No…no…no," Nati knew that only a few more moments of pressure and stimulation would bring her over the edge. Rau moved Nati's hair aside, biting into the flesh of her shoulder. The small pain spurred her on, helping her concentrate and continue through Ania's long plateau before orgasm.

Suddenly, Ania erupted. Her hips bucked and her legs thrashed, sending the Twins (who were likely not concentrating on their tasks but rather on each other) sprawling. Nati held her and anchored her, as she shattered and cried out her ecstasy. Rau continued to pound her from behind, as Nati felt Ania tremble with aftershocks. From the intensity of sucking to soft licks, Nati knew to ease off as the climax ended though it was difficult to concentrate as well as she wished when she was being fucked mercilessly. Rau must have watched Ania release, for he too was quickly overtaken. He withdrew and came with a muffled roar on Nati's backside, and Nati panted as she gently slipped her wet fingers from Ania's sex and reached them up to place in Cellet's mouth. Cellet suckled contentedly, her impossibly arranged teeth scraping at odd angles. Nati finally looked up at Ania's flushed face.

Ania's legs remained widespread, with Nati between them as the caretaker behind her head carefully released her wrists and rubbed circulation back into them. Ania lay still, her eyes slowly opened to gaze at Nati. The relaxed ease in her features was unmistakable, and new. In a drowsy voice, she mumbled,

"Thank you."

Nati smiled and kissed her gently, knowing there was much in this life she could not do —for Ania or anyone else, but cherishing the fact that she had done what she could.

No Escape
By Marie Rebelle

Nicki pulled into the parking lot, and looked at the building in front of her. It did not look at all like a hotel, which was where she thought she had to go. At last she and Craig, her husband, had found time in their busy schedules to take an afternoon off to meet each other away from home for some sexy fun. With the kids growing up and at home at the strangest times during the day, there was no chance for them to have their naughty fun at home. Craig had told her that he would take care of all the details. All she had to do was to "bring her pretty ass to the party," as he had put it.

She double-checked the address in the text message that Craig had sent her. She was definitely at the right place. Nicki parked her car in one of the available spots, grabbed the bag she had on the back seat and got out. Inside, she walked towards the counter where a stern-looking woman typed away at a computer.

"Ah, Mrs. Carter. You can go right to room eleven, it's down the hallway. Mr. Carter is waiting for you there," the woman spoke before Nicki could utter a word. Nicki nodded and smiled, turned around and walked down the faintly lit hallway. She stopped in front of a black door with "11" painted on it. Should she just walk in? Should she knock? She decided to knock.

"Come on in, silly," her husband said as he opened the door. "You did not have to knock."

He pulled her close, and kissed her softly. Her lips parted under his, inviting his tongue in to softly touch hers. When they stopped kissing, he pulled her into the room with him. Nicki stopped in her tracks when she saw the room. This was not a hotel—this was a dungeon! Not only was there a bed in the room, but there was a St. Andrew's Cross on the wall, chains hanging from beams in the ceiling, a massage table with hooks all around for rope to be tied to and a sex sling hanging from the ceiling in the corner. Against the wall hung an array of different objects, such as ticklers, whips, paddles and canes.

"I thought you might like this more than a hotel room," Craig said.

A smile formed on Nicki's face, and she nodded.

"And," Craig continued. "I have a surprise for you later."

Nicki quickly took a shower in the small bathroom, before she walked back to where Craig waited. She remained naked, and Craig told her to get onto her hands and knees on the massage table. She sighed as he poured an ample amount of lubricant between her cheeks. One finger entered her, and she pushed back against it. More lubricant followed, and he added a second finger to the first. After he had poured more lubricant, he slowly and patiently pushed a butt plug into her. Nicki knew her husband well enough to understand that at some point this afternoon, they would have anal sex.

Craig helped her off the table and briefly pulled her close to him, before he turned her around to face away from him. Nicki sighed when the first piece of rope touched her wrists, which she now held behind her back. She loved the way that the rope seemed to hug her body, it comforted her and calmed her. Whenever Craig tied her up, she relaxed fully and surrendered to what he wanted to do to her. Rope always caused her submissive nature to surface immediately, made her more obedient and at peace with herself. She smiled as he walked around her to tie a chest harness around her body, with rope running above and below her full breasts. The rope ran around her upper arms too and when Craig was done, she could not move her arms anymore.

Next, Craig tied rope around her hips. Only once before had he tied harnesses around both her hips and her chest, Nicki wondered where he was going with this. The plug moved inside her, making a twitch of horniness rush through her crotch. She loved being tied up, but at this moment she would have loved it more to be fucked by her husband. Craig ran the rope around her left thigh twice, and then tied it to the rope around her hips. He repeated the process on the right, and ended by tying a knot in the middle in front of her crotch. Nicki closed her eyes when he ran the piece of rope around her back, just above her hip and back towards the middle knot in the front. He repeated this and completed the hip harness by tying a firm knot in the front, and working away all the loose ends of the rope.

Nicki still had her eyes closed, concentrating on the firmness of the two harnesses around her body. She allowed her shoulders to relax into the rope and when she moved slightly, the hip harness reminded her that she was tied. The hip harness did not restrict any of her movements like the chest harness did, but it was tight and she felt it with every move she made. Nicki opened her eyes when Craig ran several strands of rope around her back, and tied a firm knot in front of her body. Then he tied rope around both her ankles, and slightly above her knees. By now Nicki understood that Craig wanted to try something new with the rope. Her suspicions were confirmed, when he walked her towards the heavy steel chains hanging from the ceiling.

"Lean back," he said running a piece of rope through the knot in the front of the chest harness, and a sturdy carbine hook in the chain above her. Nicki leaned back, but still supported some of her weight on her feet. Craig tied rope to the hip harness, and pulled her hips up until her body hung horizontally on the chains. For good measure he also tied a third rope to the knot on the rope around her middle. Nicki's legs still hung down, but did not touch the floor anymore. She relaxed her neck and hung her head backwards, savoring the feeling of surrender. Her husband pulled her legs up by the rope above her knees, and tied them in place. Her knees were bent and pulled up higher than her body, and her legs were spread wide. She was exposed to Craig's eyes, and ready to receive what he wanted to give her. Finally, Craig tied her feet to chains, which caused her to hang steady in one position.

"That's it," he said as he walked around her. "Now I can do whatever I want to you."

He ran his hand along the side of her body, walked around her and continued on to her other side. When he walked around for the second time, he paused to cover her eyes with a blindfold. Instantly all sensations intensified by tenfold: the rope hugging her, his hand touching her, her exposed cunt and her submission. Craig stood between her legs and touched her cunt, slowly pushing a finger inside.

"You are wet and ready, sweetheart. Are you horny?"

"Yes," Nicki said blushing a bit. "I am."

Against her expectations, Craig positioned himself between her legs. Firmly, he sucked on her clitoris. It did not take her long to climax, with his mouth still covering her button. He alternated between licking softly and sucking hard, until she climaxed again. The position she hung in did not give her any room to move, as yet another climax followed with his lips still tightly sucking her clitoris and his finger deep inside her.

There was a knock at the door. Embarrassment! Shock! Nicki tried to wriggle and close her legs, but only managed to swing slightly in her suspension. She wanted to speak, but Craig had already walked to the door and opened it. A male voice filled the room, and a shiver of shock ran down her spine when she heard her husband's words.

"She's ready for you."

"Now that looks delicious," a familiar voice said.

"I invited Sean over for our little party, Nicki, and he has been looking forward to taking..." Craig chuckled. "advantage of the situation."

"I have indeed," Sean said. "I have indeed, and you look so inviting!"

Nicki shivered with delight when Sean cupped her breast in one of his big hands, and Craig's hand cupped the other one.

Sensory overload captured Nicki, as hands moved all over her body and she could not tell who touched her where. They surrounded her, touching every inch of her flesh that was not covered by the ropes. When they stopped, Sean stood between her legs, resting his hands on her thighs and Craig stood by her head. He bent down and kissed her.

"Relax and enjoy, darling," he said.

Nicki's nipples were hard. Sean's hands burned the insides of her thighs. She imagined him looking down on her exposed cunt, and her nipples hardened even more.

Sean looked at Nicki's spread pussy and kissed her thighs, before moving to her clitoris which he sucked firmly into his mouth. Nicki breathed in deep, but was interrupted when Craig pushed his cock into her mouth. He cradled the sides of her head to keep her steady, and moved his hard member in and out of her mouth. Sean stopped sucking her, unbuckled his belt, unzipped his pants and let them fall to his feet. Slowly, he pushed his cock into her waiting wetness.

Nicki felt the strain of the ropes against her shoulders, as well as a tingling sensation in her fingers. She knew she could not stay hanging from the ropes for too much longer. Eagerly she sucked and licked her husband's cock, while Sean fucked her. The men held her between them—Craig with his hands on either side of her head, and Sean holding onto her thighs. Nicki's orgasm was building, as she noticed that Craig was getting close too. She climaxed moments before he spurted his hot come into her mouth. Only a small drop of his semen escaped her mouth. Sean pulled his cock from her, not ready to come yet.

"Craig," Nicki said. "My hands are getting numb."

Both men quickly untied her, and helped her towards the bed. They massaged her arms for a while to get the blood flowing again, but then put cuffs back around her wrists and lead her towards the massage table. Craig looped a piece of rope through the steel rings on each of the leather wrist cuffs, and tied Nicki's arms sideways to the table. Her chest rested flat on the narrow table, while her head hung over the edge on the other side. The table supported her upper body.

Sean returned between her legs, and his hard penis easily slipped into her waiting pussy. Nicki moaned. In this new position the plug moved around inside her even more than it had while she was suspended in the air. She wanted Sean to fuck her harder, but he moved in and out at his own pace. She glanced at her husband, who watched them while he slowly stroked his half-hard cock. Nicki knew how much he liked to watch when another man fucked her. Sean quickened his pace a bit, then suddenly pulled out of her and pushed two fingers into her pussy. He pushed those same fingers into her mouth, so she could taste her own juices, which she sucked and licked. He entered her again, fucking her until she almost climaxed, pulled out and pushed his fingers back into her and she licked her juices off his fingers again. Sean kept her on the brink of a climax indefinitely.

Her entire body screamed for release when he stopped and pulled on the plug. Slowly. Edging it out of her ass, bit by bit. She missed it instantly when it was gone. But not for long. Sean put the head of his cock against her ass, and pushed. The butt plug and lubricant had prepared her well, it only hurt a little when he slipped into her ass and filled the void the plug had left. Nicki looked at her husband, and smiled at him. Craig held his cock in front of her mouth, she eagerly took him into her mouth. Nicki was yet again overwhelmed by all of the sensation: being immobilized by the rope, sucking her husband and being fucked anally was enough to give her the release she wanted. She climaxed.

Neither of the men was done yet. Craig pulled out of her mouth, holding his cock teasingly close to her face, but not close enough for her to reach. Sean continued to move his cock in and out of her. He laughed when she tried to push back against him, and sped up his pace. Nicki groaned. When she tried to move with him, the ropes held her back. He quickened his pace again, pushing his hands under her body and squeezed her breasts. The harder he fucked her, the harder he squeezed her breasts until pain and pleasure mixed and she climaxed again. The tightening of her muscles when she climaxed gripped his hard cock in her ass until Sean moaned too and fucked her harder. His cock contracted inside her, just before he spurted hot come deep into her dark hole.

Nicki's ass was filled with the semen of another

man, and her pussy ached to be touched. Her husband untied her hands, while their visitor took a shower. Nicki wondered what else they had planned for her. She was so horny and all she wanted was yet another release. She did not care how she reached it, as long as it happened.

"Suck me," her husband said, standing next to the bed where she now sat.

She squatted in front of him, her legs spread. Nicki took his half-hard penis into her mouth. There was the familiar taste of his pre-cum. Her lips closed around his member, as she sucked and moved her head backwards. She licked the head of his cock, moving her hand up and down his shaft and opened her mouth to take more of him in again. Sucking. Licking. He grew harder in her mouth.

"Get on the bed, on your knees," Craig ordered.

She thought that Craig would fuck her, but was surprised when she saw him go to the dresser. He walked over with a vibrator, and pressed against her ass where come still leaked out of her. He stretched her hole again, fucking her with the vibrator. Nicki moaned as another climax overwhelmed her. More, she thought, I want more. Her shoulders rested on the bed, her ass in the air. She begged Craig to fuck her, almost screamed when his cock slipped into her pussy with the vibrator still filling her ass. With her husband pushing in and out of her pussy and at the same time the vibrator pushing into her ass, the sensation was like having two cocks inside of her.

Suddenly Craig grabbed her hair and pulled. Her back arched, and her tits protruded towards the naked man standing in front of her. Sean returned from the shower, got onto the bed, he sucked her nipples and bit them. He knew her well enough to know that Nicki liked a bit of roughness in her sex play. Nicki's moans turned from soft to loud: her husband pounded her pussy, the vibrator filled her ass and her tits were being bitten. A fire burned deep inside her, promising more than only an orgasm. It burned intensely, and she knew it could only be extinguished by one of her body-consuming orgasms.

But something was missing. She needed more, wanted more. Nicki moved her hand to her pussy, but Craig grabbed her wrist and held her arm behind her. She supported herself on one arm, and could not move. Sean turned on his side, just reaching her clitoris with his tongue. The fire in her was fed. Craig slowed his pace, allowing her to enjoy him a bit longer. He turned the knob on the back of the vibe, starting the vibrations. Gradually he quickened his pace again. Sean stopped his licking attempts, replacing his tongue with his finger and slowly circled her clitoris. With his other hand, Sean pinched her nipples, first the one, then the other.

"Fuck me," Nicki sighed.

Her husband did, along with the vibrator.

"Pinch harder," Nicki begged.

Sean hurt her nipples. Pinching them, pulling them.

Her husband pulled her head back a little more.

It hurt. Her nipples and hair being pulled, hurt. It was good. Being hurt. Being fucked. Being pleased by two men.

"Fuck!"

She pleaded.

"Me!"

Sean's hand on her clitoris had a firm touch. Craig fucked her hard, and her ass was filled. A tingling sensation started simultaneously in Nicki's toes and nipples. The tingling surged through her body, towards her pussy. Her pussy muscles contracted, tightening around her husband's cock. Craig moaned as he emptied his balls into his wife's cunt, his penis contracted inside her, he grunted and his warm come filled Nicki.

Words tumbled from her lips.

"I am going to come. I am going to come. Oh god. Oh my god. I am..."

At last she found the relief she begged for.

"I."

She moaned.

"Am."

She grunted.

"Coming."

Love on the Line
By Vita Perez

"Watch your step, Beautiful."

Nina smiled at the older man. Stepping around a puddle, she hastened her step making her way up 40th Street against the frigid wind. Her ankle-length wool coat could only help but so much, against the plummeting temperatures of January in New York City. Under her coat she wore only a black lace bra, and a G-string with matching garters and thigh-highs which probably didn't help her current arctic state.

Nina felt tingling deep in her core, at the thought of what awaited her. With each step she took closer to the hotel, she felt her excitement and arousal rise. Feeling the tug of her garters as she walked, she flushed at the thought of Damon's first glance at her lingerie. Never in her life had she felt so sexy and reckless. At thirty-five, she was on her way to her first rendezvous with a lover. Sure she'd had relationships and boyfriends, but nothing like this. Her anticipation was almost enough to keep her warm as she trekked to the hotel…but only barely.

She turned down her collar as she stepped into the lobby of the Elements Hotel. The sudden blast of warmth took her breath away.

Am I really going through with this? Am I ready for this?

Nina knew once she slept with Damon there was no going back. She held the room key in her pocket, he had it messengered to her apartment earlier in the day. The hotel was very zen in its green and grey decor, with accents of river rocks and bamboo throughout the lobby. Moving quickly, she past the reception desk and turned the corner. Standing before the elevator banks, Nina let out the breath she hadn't realized she was holding until that moment. She got into the car with a family and an older couple, moved to the back of the elevator. By the time the elevator reached her floor, she was alone staring at her blurred reflection in the elevator door. She barely recognized herself, and quickly raced out before the doors had opened fully.

Nina found the room easily, but paused in front of the door. Even as she gripped the keycard in her hand, she questioned whether she should knock or just walk in. Her sudden nervousness at what awaited her behind that door rendered her petrified and unable to decide.

Damon Green. Just the thought of him left her feeling flushed. They had met six months before at a three-day conference in Florida. She had just ordered a glass of white wine at the hotel bar she sat at with her longtime friend in the industry, Lettie Peña, when she turned to find him smiling at her.

"Damon this is my good friend, Nina Sanchez."

They shook hands, and she did her best not to stare or drool. He was African-American with a warm honey complexion and dark almond eyes. His chiseled jaw was accented by a perfectly trimmed beard, and a sexy-as-hell bald head. He was gorgeous. With his tailored slate wool suit, lavender shirt and a charcoal tie, he stood out in the room. There were more than a few women who'd taken notice of him in the bar, and there she was shaking his hand unable to manage more than a smile. To say she felt flustered just looking at him was an understatement, but it only lasted a moment. She quickly checked herself, remembering professional men as gorgeous as Damon did not go for women like her. They were attracted to women like Lettie: tall with toned athletic figures and long glossy straight hair. They were not attracted to women like herself, who would be considered more full figured: big breasts and full hips. Her wavy hair was in a slicked back ponytail that reached the middle of her back—the only way she could manage to tame her reckless locks in the unrelenting Miami humidity.

Once that realization hit her, she was able to fall into an easy conversation with him. And damn if he wasn't just as charming, as he was handsome. The conversation began easily enough about the conference for freelance recruiters but as the night went on, conversation turned to their shared interests. From Basquiat to Mapplethorpe, they compared notes on contemporary and modern art. Nina found herself taking mental notes of his preferences.

After that night, they found themselves circling back to one another other throughout the remainder of the conference. On the last day, they exchanged cards making promises to keep in touch. About a week later, much to her surprise he kept his promise with a simple text:

Hey there stranger.

Now she stood before the hotel room, suddenly unsure if she was in over her head and unable to bring herself to put the key in the door. Over the past few months, his flirtation had become something much more. It was clear he wanted her, wanted to fulfill her fantasies and more. But was she ready for that? To say that the texts and suggestions of what he wanted to do to her was so much more than her vanilla experiences could ever have conjured, was an understatement. She shook her dark hair behind her, and lifted her chin.

What the hell do you have to lose?

Nina raised a shaky hand, and knocked a bit more forcefully than she intended. She heard movement within, and almost turned tail and ran back to the elevator. But she held her ground. Damon was suddenly before her holding the room door open, barefoot. He had taken off his tie and unbuttoned his dress shirt, his sculpted chest and abs were bared to her.

"Hey you. Afraid to use the key, huh?" he said with a smile as he stepped back to allow her to pass.

Her heart raced. He was even more beautiful than she remembered. Even at 5'8" with four-inch heels, he still towered over her at 6'3". She smiled weakly, unsure how to respond. He placed the "Do Not Disturb" sign on the door handle, and closed it. Walking into the suite on shaky legs, Nina placed her bag on an armchair. A king-size bed was visible to her left, through a double-wide doorway.

"Let me take your coat." She unbuttoned it without turning to him, letting it slip past her shoulders as she turned. "I see you got the lingerie I sent you."

"I did."

Taking her coat, he tossed it on to the same chair as her bag. Damon swept her hair back off her shoulders, sending shivers down her spine as he moved around her. She faced him, and he backed her up against the closet door. Her heart pounded in her ears, from a mixture of fear and excitement. Running his fingers over her jaw as his thumb skimmed over her bottom lip, he let out a low hum of pleasure. Slowly he moved his hand further up into the nape of her neck. She licked her lips, and watched as his eyes became heavy with want. Fisting her hair lightly, he angled her ear to his lips.

"Open your mouth wider, and lick your lips again for me." She obliged drawing out the movement, reveling in his eyes locked on her mouth. "Do you know how long I've been thinking about those lips? I wanna see those pretty thick lips…" He tilted his head, eyes locked on her mouth. "All over me."

Her body ignited. Wet did not even begin to describe what he'd just done to her with just his words. Her knees felt weak at the mental image of placing her lips over his most delicate parts.

"Are you ready for me?" he questioned.

"Yes." She panted as he tightened the grip in her hair. Kissing her hard, his tongue plunged into her mouth finding her own. Nina felt on the verge of coming just from that penetration alone. He broke away from her, leading her to the doorway of the bedroom. Leaving her standing there alone, he quickly returned with red satin ties in his hands.

"Do you trust me?"

She stared into his eyes, nodding.

"Yes."

He bound first one wrist and then the other with the opposite end of the red sash. Damon hooked the loose end between her hands, over a hook above the door frame. He walked around her, taking in her position and his hand caressed her ass as he did. Standing behind her, he pulled her hair way from her face, fisting it he ran his tongue over her neck. Shivers climbed up her spine, and he spanked her. His hands moved from one cheek to the other in quick movements. The only sounds in the room were the smacks of flesh as he made contact with her buttocks, and her moans of pleasure.

Damon stopped, and walked over to the champagne chilling in a bucket. He poured a glass, and sipped it as he watched her. Taking an ice cube between his lips, he bent behind her. Slowly he traced all the areas he'd spanked, with the ice cube between his lips. Once melted, he kissed and licked her cheeks. Spreading her legs, he moved her -string to the side and he kissed the lips of her sex devouring every bit of her. His hands moved up and down her calves as he took her clit between his lips, sucking and licking until she came screaming his name over and over again. Hanging limp from her bindings, he once again stood behind her and she leaned back against him as he cupped her breasts.

"That was just a taste."

His husky voice growled in her ear. He pinched her nipples as she moved her hips, grinding against his rock-hard erection pressed against her behind. Unhooking the red sash from above her head, he untied her hands. Damon lifted her with ease, and carried her to the bed. He rubbed the feeling back into her arms and hands, as his mouth found hers and she moaned into his kiss. He continued until she writhed under him, her legs wrapped around his waist.

"You ready for round two baby?" he whispered into her ear.

"Oh yes," she answered with a smile.

He stood up and brought her glass of champagne, which she sipped, as she watched him undress. His body was lean and muscular. She smiled and saluted him with her glass, as he dropped his pants and boxer shorts. Nina barely recognized herself with him. With him she was sexy, confident, but more than that she felt desirable. And it felt glorious.

"Will you come take off mine now?"

She asked as she placed her glass on the nightstand. He swiftly pulled her legs close to him, causing her to squeal. He grabbed the fabric of her G-string from between her legs and with a wink, ripped it off of her.

"I'll buy you another."

She lay beneath him in her bra and garters, her sex exposed to him. His gaze traveled over every inch of her body.

"I have fantasized, dreamed and wished of having you like this since the first night I meet you." He slid his hands under her thighs, until they rested under her butt. Slowly he bent as he kissed her softly, tasting her, savoring her lips and leaving her breathless.

This is perfection, she thought to herself. His kisses intensified as he caressed her body. He removed her bra, his mouth on her taut nipple. He parted her labia, plunging first one and then a second finger into her. Nina writhed against his hands, she was so close.

"*Mi tesoro*, my treasure, please…I need to feel you…"

She lost her ability to speak as his thumb circled

her clit, at the same moment his teeth grazed her aching nipple. Pulling away from her, he quickly put on a condom and moved over her.

"You ready for me, Beautiful?"

"More than you know."

Her last word caught in her throat, and she hoped he didn't notice. In that moment, she knew this was not just sex for her. Yes, they flirted and shared endless innuendos and sexually-laced quips, but they also talked about their lives. His texts were the first thing she looked for in the morning, and the last thing she saw at night. She'd told him everything about herself in their late-night chats and he did the same. She knew his ambitions, knew he wanted leave Philadelphia and move to New York. That his favorite color is purple, and he hates peanut butter.

He kissed her softly pulling her from her thoughts.

"What's wrong, Beautiful? You look so serious all of a sudden."

She shook her head, and pulled him into another kiss, afraid to speak. He eased into her, filling her inch by inch. They moved as one, savoring the moment. So different from how they began, but no less wonderful. He took his time and she did the same, running her hands over the hard lines of his muscles. Their slow lovemaking gained momentum, and her orgasm built until it exploded. Damon grabbed her hips, thrusting into her over and over again as she called his name. Waves of pleasure washed over her, making him come soon after her.

Hours passed, and Nina never felt more alive. They ordered room service, ate, laughed and talked about everything and nothing. Made love again. And again. By 4:00 in the morning, she knew she had to leave. He had to get ready to catch a 6:30 train back to Philly.

She dressed in the leggings and sweater she had tucked in her oversized purse.

"Damn if you don't look just as sexy in those leggings as you do without them." He said as he nuzzled her neck.

"I don't know if I can go back to just texts and the occasional phone call now." Nina said with a smile. She felt him freeze for a second, before he kissed her neck and pulled away. Her stomach twisted into a knot.

"Let me pay for your cab home. It's too dark and cold for you to take the subway home alone."

He tucked forty dollars in her coat, as he helped her into it.

"Text me when you get home, Beautiful."

He cupped her face and kissed her slowly at first, the heat between them rapidly building. He pulled away looking as breathless as she felt.

"You better go."

They shared one last hug, and he watched her from the door until the elevator came. She waved and watched as he closed his door.

***

Nina unwrapped her scarf, handing it along with her coat to the receptionist. She'd been called in to meet with the HR heads for CronoLyte, home to her latest freelance project. She was helping the rapidly expanding tech company build their research department. They wanted the best and brightest in the industry, and were willing to pay for it. She'd been at it for three months and had already placed two of the five open positions. It was taking her longer than she'd hoped to place the posts. Her gut told her they were going to pull her from the contract, but she was prepared. She had reached out to a few contacts, and had stuff set up to wow them. The commission alone from this project would be able to carry her for six months, even without her per diem.

She smoothed her dress over her thighs, as she waited in one of the posh leather armchairs. Her dress bunched on her, as she'd lost more weight. Even though she'd sworn to Lettie it was just her imagination, when she saw her for brunch last week. It'd been about three months since that night with Damon. He'd sent a quick text to him once she got home and he sent her one once he got back to Philly. Then it seemed everything changed. He was consistent for about a week or so, then his texts came fewer and fewer. When she called him on it, he said he was making big moves, and would make it up to her once he had everything nailed down. He claimed he would come see her, and then would go radio silent for days. This latest stretch was six weeks and counting.

Nina had become a workaholic to stop herself from thinking about Damon. She got up at 6:00 in the morning, and went to bed one in the morning. She worked until she was bleary-eyed: setting up conference calls and working on multiple freelance projects at once. Lettie told her she was burning herself out, and that's why she was coming up short on filling the other three positions.

"You probably sound desperate."

Nina choked on Lettie's words. Maybe that's what scared Damon away? Or maybe she just thought they had more than they really were? She got carried away thinking his lust was love. But when she closed her eyes at night, she knew in her heart it was more. They'd made love, it wasn't just sex. But in the light of day, her empty message box brought her back to reality.

"Ms. Sanchez, you can go right in. They are ready for you."

Alright chica, it's show time. Time to put it all on the line.

Nina walked into the room, and shook hands with the HR executives. It had been a while since she'd sat face to face with them. The two directors of HR were named Johnson; one fair-haired and the other dark. The fair-haired Johnson was in his late fifties, and the other mid-thirties. She could never remember their first names, so she called them both Mr. Johnson. The VP of HR, Felice Dumont, a fifty-something French ex-pat, was an expert in global relations. Nina liked her friendly and personal approach. She knew if she was going to work this meeting to her benefit, she was going to need Felice on her side.

"Gentlemen, Ms. Dumont…"

"Ms. Sanchez, we have one more person joining us." Ms. Dumont said as there was a knock at the door.

"Oh, " Nina said as she turned toward the door smiling.

"Come in. Nina Sanchez, this is Damon Green."

Nina sat speechless, her smile frozen on her face. She felt a flush rise across her face and neck.

"Nina and I actually know each other," Damon said.

All eyes turned to Nina, as she fought down the urge to run out of the room.

"Yes, we met at a conference for freelance recruiters last fall in Miami." She said curtly, with a thin-lipped smile. "So…shall we begin since we're all here?"

Nina lifted her pen to take notes but her hands trembled so badly, she quickly placed them in her lap. Damon took the seat next to her, letting it roll closer to her as he turned to face Ms. Dumont and the Johnsons. She could see him out of the corner of her eye, as she struggled to focus her attention on the woman before her. Her mind raced, as she struggled to focus on the conversation. Why was he there? What was he doing in New York?

Focus chica, focus.

"…because of this merger and the need for ten more high-level coders and technicians, we would like you to work as a team. With that being said we, of course, will still honor your original contact Nina plus an additional percentage to the commission bonus for taking on this added project."

"Work together?" Nina could barely hear herself over the pounding of her heart beating in her ears.

"I think it's a great idea. And I personally can't wait to get started and show you what we can do," Damon said.

The Johnsons went into details of what they were looking for, and Nina fought to keep her face neutral. Damon knew how much this freelance gig meant to her. It was not only a good payoff for this year, but it meant potential referrals and future work. To say no to working with him, meant she was throwing it all away. Her stomach felt like lead.

"Nina?" She looked at Ms. Dumont. "My apologies we jumped ahead, and did not give a chance to weigh in. Are you open to taking on this additional project?"

She could lie and say she'd already lined up a project, but she knew even if the Johnsons didn't see through the lie, Ms. Dumont would and she was the one that counted. All eyes were on her. She turned for a second to Damon, her heart clenched and she looked away.

"Of course."

"Wonderful!"

The next twenty minutes passed for Nina in a blur. She thanked Ms. Dumont as she passed her a portfolio on the project. They all stood to say their goodbyes. She thanked Mrs. Dumont, and shook her hand quickly noticing Damon was in deep conversation with the younger Johnson. She used the moment to make a quiet exit.

Rushing over to the receptionist for her coat, Nina asked her to hurry as she was late for another meeting. She caught a brief glimpse of Damon making his way around the corner as the elevator doors closed.

With a quick exit from the building, she hopped into the first cab she saw. As the taxi pulled away from the curb, Nina sank into the backseat and closed her eyes. While she thought for sure she would have burst into tears the moment she was out of there, she instead felt sick to her stomach. How do you work with the man you're in love with, knowing that he doesn't love you? Especially if you know he used you for sex, and then blew you off.

Nina had the cabbie drop her off at Union Square, and she hopped on the train from there. An hour later, she flopped onto her sofa in her favorite yoga shorts and oversized, lived-in Knicks T-shirt. Take-out Chinese food for dinner sat on the coffee table before her, though she knew she probably wouldn't eat it. What she would eat, was the extra-large bag of popcorn open on her lap. Staring absently at the TV, she popped a few kernels into her mouth. Missed texts from Damon blinked across her phone, but couldn't bring herself to read them. What could he possibly say…*oopsy I forgot your number for a few weeks there*?

She picked up her phone more than once to call her sister Diana, but chickened out. As much as she wanted to call her sister or even one of her cousins and tell them everything, she couldn't bring herself to pick up the phone. She couldn't bear to hear even one of them ask her what she was thinking. Damon had been her special thing that she didn't share with anyone. She had wanted him all to herself. Now it just seemed like she was hiding a dirty secret.

A quarter of the way into the popcorn bag, she heard a knock at her door. Cursing inwardly, she remembered she was supposed to return the hammer she borrowed a few weeks before to the super. She'd been avoiding him in the hall for the past week and a half. Even worse was she had no idea where she'd put the damn hammer, and could not remember for the life of her what it looked like to buy a replacement. *Could this day get any worse?*

"Who is it?"

"It's Damon. Nina please open up, I need to talk to you."

So apparently it could get worse. Why couldn't he have been the super?

"There's nothing to talk about Damon, I got the hint. We can review the project via e-mail on Monday. Have a goodnight," she said curtly. Her knees shook under her, as she braced herself against the door frame to steady herself.

Just walk away, please just walk away.

"I'm not leaving. Let me in," he sighed. She felt the sting of tears which had refused to fall all day, deciding to now make their appearance at the most inopportune time. "Nina, I know I fucked this up so bad. I had this great plan, that in my head, made so much sense. But when I saw your face today I realized how wrong I was. Please Nina, just give me five minutes."

Her heart broke all over again. But if she was going to have to work with him to keep her commission and connections, she would have to face him eventually. Nina took several deep breaths and once she was sure potential tears were finally in check, she unlocked the door.

"You have five minutes, then you have to go."

She stepped aside and let him in, then stood with her back to the door and crossed her arms across her chest. "I'm waiting, your time is ticking."

"Baby…" He moved to put his arms around her, but she threw up her hands to ward him off. "Okay." He stepped back, "I never meant to hurt you."

Nina rolled her eyes.

"I went back to Philly, determined to figure out a way to move here and be here with you," he continued. "Remember I told you I had something big in the works? I thought I could work everything out, sell my place. Set up a few placements, and surprise you with me here in the city."

Nina looked at him in disbelief.

"You must really think I'm stupid," she said as anger replaced her heartache. "You know what? I know you must think I'm stupid. Why else would you have the balls to show up here after the way you've treated me?"

"It's not like that Nina. I don't think you're stupid, if anything I'm the stupid one."

"Why are you here?"

"Do you remember the last time I saw you, and you said you didn't know if you could go back to phone calls and texts?"

"Let me guess, you decided to make it come true my cutting off both?"

"No…no," he shook his head. "When you said that, I realized I couldn't go back to just texts and phone calls either."

"So you stopped doing both? If this is your way of saying sorry…you suck at it."

"I went home, sold my place and started looking for a place in New York. In my mind, you knew how much I wanted to be with you and because I told you I was working on some stuff, I thought you would be okay if I wasn't around for a few."

"Six weeks?"

Damon cringed at her words.

"I know you have every right not to believe me."

"You need to go." Nina turned to open the door. Damon moved behind her and placed his hands on the door, his chest was hard against her back.

"I fucked up, I know I fucked up. But you have to know, I am in love with you. When I heard from CronoLyte looking for another freelancer…I jumped at it. I knew it would freak you out that they called in another person. I thought me taking the post would be the best of both worlds."

Nina felt her resolve waning. He said he loved her, words she so desperately wanted to hear.

"Look at me, Nina." He turned her around, and his eyes searched hers. He cupped her face, and tears fell as he kissed her. "You are all I want. That night with you made me want a life with you."

He wrapped his arms around her. His soft kisses became more urgent, as his tongue found hers and she melted into him. As much as she knew she shouldn't, she believed him, needed to believe him.

They made their way to the bedroom. Slowly he undressed her, kissing every inch of her bare skin as he uncovered it. While he undressed, she kissed and caressed him. Naked on the bed, bodies moving as one, they paused for her to get a condom. Damon entered Nina smoothly to the hilt, making her cry out. She felt raw as ached for all of him, her tears returned and he kissed them away.

"I will spend the rest of my life making this up to you." he promised, and she buried her head in his chest. "Nina look at me." She forced her eyes to meet his. "I love you."

"I love you too."

Her orgasm hit her with a force so intense, she

felt as though she would shatter to pieces. He continued to move within her until it built again, and as she climaxed for a second time and he came with her calling her name.

After she pulled the covers around them, and Damon told her every detail of what he'd done to get back to her. When he was done she kissed him and said,

"Say it again."

"I love you. I love you. I love you."

She took a deep breath and closed her eyes.

Time to put it your heart on the line.

She pulled the covers tighter around them, and slept.

Birthday Knots
By Cheryl Kaye

Are you sure that's what you want? I mean I know you say you want it, but it was my idea originally and I don't want you to ask for it to please me. This is the sort of thing you need to be sure of. You can't just do it on a whim." I smiled at John, and stroked his bare chest. "You think about it a bit longer. Your birthday is still over a month away. There's plenty of time."

"I don't want to think about it any longer. It's all I've thought about for weeks, ever since you told me that little story. You asked what I wanted for my birthday, well that's what I want." He caught my hand, and brought it to his mouth kissing my palm, then my wrist and worked his way up my arm. "Please - Miss. It really is what I want."

He kissed me, one of those long slow kisses that melted my insides and turned my brain to mush. When we finally stopped kissing, I reached over to grab my laptop from beside the bed.

"Ok, then we have some research to do."

***

"What about this one? He's nice…oh no hang on, he's straight. Why bloody send us a message if you don't want to 'do the guy?' Idiot." I sat on the sofa with my laptop open on my knees, while John made dinner. "Why the hell can't people read our post properly before replying? It's not like we don't clearly state we're looking for a bi-man. I'm beginning to think they're a myth... or they're too smart to be on this stupid website."

I deleted each message that said the guy (and occasional girl) doesn't have sex with men or women, and started to worry we wouldn't find anyone.

"Stop that. It's going to work out. You know these sites are always full of time-wasters. You just have to be patient, we'll find someone."

I stuck my tongue out at him, "If we build it, he will come."

"Yeah, pretty much," He laughed. "Read me some more."

I scrolled through the messages, deleting the rejects until I had a very short list of actual contenders that I read out loud.

"This one sounds good. He's a consultant…not really sure what that means, but he travels a lot. He's not local, but is often here on business. Or this one, he's a yoga teacher and performance poet. Oooh, he's only 5'6. That's not much taller than me. This guy is tall, a personal trainer and mentions pro-wrestlers... not sure about that. There's a doctor though he seems a little boring but I guess we're not picking them for dinner conversation are we? Shall I message them all back, ask for more details and a photo? Do we want to see what they look like?"

John looked at me.

"I know it's kind of superficial but yeah, I really want to see what they look like before we decide. And scratch the yoga guy, we definitely want someone big…I mean taller."

He blushed, and I smiled at him.

"Big is good too."

He sat down next to me, and I turned the laptop so he could see the screen properly.

"I like the doctor and the consultant based purely on their photos, what do you think?" I have a feeling you might prefer the paramedic." I pulled up each photo, putting them into a grid so we could see them all together.

"How do I know which is which?"

I laughed.

"You don't, that's the point. You're picking purely on looks. Pick two or three and so we can check their profiles, and see who we like together."

"Ah got you….Let's see. Not that one. And definitely not that one, he looks a bit terrifying." I deleted each picture as John dismissed it, "I like him. Oooh, and him. Maybe him... actually on second thoughts, not him. But maybe him."

I couldn't help but smile at John's excitement.

"Well, you did pick the paramedic, and the consultant... and your maybe was the doctor. The scary one was the personal trainer." I giggled, and took a deep breath trying to reign it in. "Now we need to pick one."

"Well, we both liked the consultant. Plus he's not local so chances of bumping into him somewhat are slim. And if we want to do it again sometime, it would still be a possibility. Yeah, he's good. Let's find out when he's in town next, and if he is really interested.

***

I looked at John as I pulled my skirt on and tucked in my shirt. His eyes flicked up and down my figure, I grinned at him as I slipped my shoes on.

"I shouldn't be long…although you never know. Be good."

I grabbed my bag as I headed to the door, then I had an idea. Pulling out my phone, I turned back around and held it up so I could snap a photo. He looked so good on his knees, his arms stretched above his head. I had the rope running from his wrists over the curtain pole, and down to his ankles. I'd allowed a little bit of slack, but it essentially held him in place as he faced the window without quite touching it. If his arms got tired, he could move his ankles together and lower them a few inches inches at the most.

When I pulled open the door and flipped the sign to "Do Not Disturb," I had a perfect profile view of him looking out of the window. I stepped out and closed the door behind me, smiling as I walked down the corridor. He was already getting hard. He really loved the idea of being "on show."

***

I sat at the hotel bar, stirring my drink with a cocktail stick topped with an olive. In the mirror behind the bar, I could watch people come and go. As soon as I saw him, I knew it was him: tall, dark hair, and wearing a suit so perfect it had to be tailor-made for him. He was toned enough you could tell he worked out, but not so much that it was all he did. I practically drooled in my drink. He'd scanned the bar from the door, and approached a few women sitting alone before he ended up standing next to me. He ordered an old-fashioned, and I swiveled around to face him.

"Funny, you don't look like an old-fashioned guy."

He turned to look at me. His eyes took in the diamond on my ring finger, and lingered on my cleavage before he met my eyes and smiled.

"Well, it's a good drink. I'm all for trying new things, but nothing has beaten it yet. I'm Sam."

I grinned at him.

"Lucky me, I'm Cara."

Relief crossed his face, as his eyes flicked over my body again. We chatted easily, flirting clearly second nature to us both. We laughed and joked through our drinks.

"Just wondering, is your husband going to join us? I mean that was what we discussed, right?"

He looked slightly awkward as he asked, and I had to laugh.

"Well, no. He won't be joining us for a drink. He's a little tied up at the moment."

I waited for his reaction.

It takes a minute then he blushed and grinned.

"Ah right. Ok then."

I pulled out my phone to show him the photo.

"He's waiting at the hotel. You can still walk away, no hard feelings." I swallowed the last of my drink, and watched his face carefully. "Or you can follow me."

I slid off my seat, grabbed my bag and walked to the door without looking to see if he was behind me.

He caught up just in time to open the door for me. With a little bob of his head, he smiled.

"I'm following your lead….Miss."

I couldn't stop the grin that spread across my face.

***

I pushed open the door of the hotel room, and John twisted to look at me. His cock was rock hard, and I saw a smear on the window from where it had touched the glass before he turned. I shook my head in mock displeasure as I stepped into the room. For a moment, I saw disappointment etched on his face until I stepped aside and Sam followed me into the room. Hunger flashed across John's face, and I knew we made the right choice.

Samclosed the door, taking in the rope and window.

"Wasn't that window clean in the photo?" he asked.

I turned around to look at him.

"Yes, it was. Looks like he got a little too excited. Why don't you get undressed and get acquainted while I go find some ice?"

I picked up the ice bucket and left.

When I opened the door, they were both naked by the window. John had shifted onto his knees, so he faced Sam with his back to the door. They turned their heads as I entered, and I saw Sam was semi-erect. John looked at me, his eyes begging and his gaze flicked over Sam's cock and back to me again.

I nodded and smiled at Sam.

"I think my boy needs to taste your cock."

Sam grinned and stepped closer to John, who opened his mouth and leaned towards him. John hesitated as Sam's cock came closer, then flicked out his tongue, swiping across it the tip, before running it over the head and and opening his mouth wider to accommodate Sam's girth. Seeing John sucking on Sam's cockhead, I felt my cunt throb in response and my panties dampened.

I caught Sam's eye.

"Maybe you should see how much he can take."

He puts his hand on John's head, moved his hips forward and pushed deeper into his mouth. He stopped and pulled back when John gagged, giving him a second to breathe. Sam pushed in again, each time managing to push a little further until John's nose touched his stomach. I saw John trying to find the right method to suck, swallow and breathe all at once. He shifted and gagged again, choking slightly which caused Sam to moan and curl his fingers in John's hair. He started to pull back, but John followed his movement and moans. John flicked his eyes in my direction and wiggled his fingers, asking permission to let them roam. I shook my head, refusing to loosen his binds so he could slip his hands out. He flexed his fingers a few times as if imaging them where he wanted them to be. I moved behind Sam grabbing his ass and holding him in place, before putting my hand over his on John's head as he moved his mouth up and down Sam's shaft.

After a minute, it's too much, and I stepped back to continue watching. Making sure I was visible to both men, I slowly slid my knickers down my hips and let them drop to the floor. Watching my John sucking Sam's cock so well made me horny. I was torn between wanting to ride John's cock while he continues to suck Sam, and just wanting to enjoy the show. There's no rush, we had all night. I sprawled on the bed, slid my hand under my skirt and gently stroked my soaking cunt. I knew it wouldn't take much to bring me to orgasm, so I circled my clit with my thumb. I saw Sam watching me, his hand still tangled in John's hair and the other resting against the window. John moved his mouth back sucking hard on the head of Sam's cock, and I saw it twitch and jump. John moaned.

"Sam, maybe you should play with your balls, that hand on the window should be kept busy."

He nodded at me.

"Yes, Miss."

He cupped his balls, rolling them in his hand before tugging gently.

When Sam groaned, I felt my orgasm building, and moved my thumb faster on my clit.

"John. Make him come for me, babe."

I moaned, writhed and moved my hand even faster on my clit. John watched me, seeing how much I enjoyed the show. He slid his lips further down Sam's cock and sucked hard. Sam grunted as he thrusted into John's mouth. John moaned when Sam came, then he swallowed hard as Sam shot hot come down his throat. John kept Sam's cock in his mouth, sucking gently as Sam leaned against the window. I came hard, moaning and looking at them. I watched as John carefully licked Sam's cock to make sure he got every drop of come, before turning to grin at me.

John slumped, the rope was the only thing holding him up. I stood up on shaky legs, and walked over to the window. I unfastened his ankles and he brought his hands down to his lap, as his butt dropped onto his feet. He looked up at me and held out his hands, I winked and unfastened one. Then taking the other end of the rope, I walked over to the bed. Still on his knees John followed me, a look of uncertainty on his face.

I stopped by the end of the bed.

"On your feet," I said.

He stood slowly, leaning on the bed as he moved his legs to get the blood flowing. I gave him a minute then tugged at the rope. "You know what to do."

We'd discussed this, but that was before he'd seen Sam--and his cock--in person. I wasn't sure if John was still going to be okay with it, but he assumed the position without hesitation. I noticed the smile on his face as John bent over the end of the bed, arms out on either side. Sam stepped to the other side of the bed, I tossed him the end of the rope before and kneeled down to get the rope when he passed it under the bed. I stood and tied the end back on John's other wrist, effectively keeping him in place on the bed.

John's gaze followed Sam, as he moved around the bed to where I stood. Sam met John's gaze, then reached for me. He kissed me hard, his tongue plundering my mouth while his hands unfastened my shirt and pushed it down my arms so it fell to the floor. Then running his hands back freely over my upper torso, he paused to unhook my bra and dropped it onto the floor with my shirt. He cup and squeeze my breast, pinching its nipple. Sam dropped to his knees, pulling me down so he still sucked at my nipple until I hissed my breath through my teeth. I put one hand on his head, as the other gripped the bed sheets and I heard John moan. He moved his hips, rubbing himself against the bedding as he watched us. Sam unzipped my skirt letting it fall to the floor, then slid his hands up my legs, nudged my knees apart and swept two fingers along my still dripping cunt. Sam stood up, grinned cheekily and sucked his fingers before leaning across the bed to kiss John.

When Sam straightened up, John looked at me with longing in his eyes.

"Please?"

I couldn't deny him. I nodded, climbed onto the bed and got in front of him not quite close enough for him to taste my cunt. I grabbed his head, curling my fingers in his hair as I turn his head toward my leg. He kissed the inside of my thigh, tasting my juices that dripped and lapping them up. His tongue moved in broad strokes making my cunt throb. He turned his head to the other thigh, and I wiggled closer. I felt him smile against my thigh, before he ran his tongue across my cunt onto the other thigh and then back to my cunt. He dropped butterfly kisses from my clit down as low as he could reach and then back up letting his tongue slip between my lips to taste me. He sucked my clit, the tip of his tongue making circles as he sucked. I moaned and wriggled under his mouth, but wanted more. I reached under the pillow, and brought out a vibrating egg and moved back slightly so I could slip it in. When I moved back towards John, I saw Sam watching us. He held his hardened cock in his hand and stroked it.

I looked back at John.

"Let's find out how good your concentration is, shall we?" I nodded at Sam. "There's lube and condoms over there."

John turned his head to glance at Sam, and tensed slightly when the cold lube is squeezed onto his ass. He looked at me, making eye contact, before continuing to lick my clit. Sam slowly massaged the lube in, spreading it down John's crack and working it into John's puckered hole. I felt rather than heard John's low moan, and gently tugged his hair reminding him of his job. He kissed my cunt again, licking at my juices and flicking his tongue against me. I knew the moment Sam eased his cock into him, because he paused though not long enough to make me tug his hair but just enough so I knew. Then he moved his mouth, sucking my clit as he moved with each of Sam's thrusts. The three of us rocked together, the low buzzing of the love egg barely audible over their grunts. I moaned and whimpered as I came over and over, while Sam thrusted steadily in and out of John's ass. Sam groaned loudly as he came, and slumped against John. We were all in a heap, panting and shaking until Sam straightened and offered to make drinks. I sat up, and untied the rope from John's wrist. It was only when he stood and stepped back, that I saw the sticky patch on the sheets where the thrusting motion and his full ass caused him to come.

Bed Knobs and Belt Buckles
By Monica Corwin

Tonight, like every other night, I waited. It was his choice to show up so I was always waiting, mostly in vain, tonight, like all the others.

As I walked back and forth across the carpet, my feet emitted soft scuffing sounds but they were negligible compared to the loud thumping of my heart in my ears. In longing, or in hope he wouldn't show, I couldn't say.

The arrangement was created months prior and only once had he actually followed through on an assignation. Yet my longing for him, something, anything, kept me tied to him, requesting to see him again and again.

He was the one that got away. We were friends once, a long time ago, and while we had a strong sexual attraction we chose not to pursue it. When we fell out of touch, I thought about him often. Finally after years of not speaking we reconnected, and discussed completing what might have been once upon a time.

Now as I paced back and forth, my chest tightened with every step. I'd known this man for years, but the thought of being in his arms made me nervous. I was older, weighed more and had grown cynical in the time we spent apart. *What if he didn't like me anymore?*

I checked my face in the mirror every time I passed it, since it was opposite the door in the living room. My hair was still braided neatly, but my eyes looked darker than their usual gray-blue with the sparse eyeliner I applied. My lips were a healthy shade of pink, flushed from biting them because of my nerves.

A soft knock interrupted my pacing across the carpet, and I froze. It took a few seconds to mentally push myself to the door. I opened it, and peeked outside. He gave me a small smile and I pulled it open, the hinges squeaked for the effort.

He looked the same as ever: the same sandy blond hair and boyish grin. His blue eyes always seemed too big for his face, but made him look more gentle, more open.

"Am I allowed to come in?" John asked.

"Of course," I chuckled, shaking myself from staring at him too hard.

I moved out of the way, ushering him inside. My heart climbed up my throat, making speaking and breathing both things of the past.

His scent caught up to me after he moved past me, he smelled exactly as he had years before. Instantly, I was transported to a time when we flirted often and touched "accidentally" as much as possible. *Why hadn't I been brave enough to make a move then?* It wouldn't happen again, I resolved, as I closed the door softly and twisted the lock.

The second my fingers left the cold steel I was

shoved against the door, trapped between his warm body and the cold wood. I didn't move, unsure of what he was about to do. There was one thing I did know, this was exactly what I had been waiting for all this time.

I inhaled sharply, trying to maintain level breath while my heart tried to climb out of my mouth. His lips moved along my ear, and he whispered,

"I want you."

All my doubts, my fears and worry were gone with those three words, and the tingling breath that followed them. He pressed his hips into my ass and I couldn't help but press back against him.

Oh, God.

His warm breath fanned along the column of my neck, and up behind my ear. I swallowed the moan that threatened to escape from me, as his lips barely pressed against the sensitive flesh along my hairline.

"Are you really here, is this really happening?" I whispered as he continued to press his growing erection into my clothed backside.

"I'm really here," he said on an exhale, so softly I almost didn't hear him.

Shock and adrenaline spiked through me as he grabbed my wrists, and pulled them above my head. The coolness of the door was now a relief to the heat enveloping me, as my arousal grew.

"I love that you wore a skirt, that will make this even better."

I didn't wear any panties, thinking it would excite him and now I knew it did. He clasped both of my wrists in one hand ripped my skirt down with the other. He rubbed my ass and legs appreciatively, before opening the button and fly on his jeans. The sound of the metal grating on metal, was a reminder he wasn't inside me yet.

"I wanted this to be softer, gentler, but I don't think I can wait," he said, I felt him pulling his erection from the opening of his pants.

"Please." I squirmed in his hands, until I felt the gentle prod of his fingers between my legs. I knew what he would find there, I was more than ready for him. I'd been ready for him for years.

"You better stop squirming or I'm going to have to tie you up." His grip tightened on my wrists.

The image was more than I could handle. I let out a moan against the door, my hot breath fanned back against my face. I counted the seconds, not even fast enough to keep up with my heartbeat pounding through my ears and shooting sparks down my nerves to my toes. As the head of him brushed against my opening I whimpered, and he groaned but then stopped.

"No, please, don't stop."

I turned my head in time to see him rip the belt from his pants with a sharp thwack. I knew what he was going do, would only amp my arousal further. He doubled his belt and wrapped the loop around my wrists, slipping the ends of the belt through the middle to create a tight hold. I'd have bruises the morning to remember him by. He held the ends high above him, he had almost a foot of height over me.

"Stop squirming or I'll make you wait longer," he growled into my ear and nipped the lobe for good measure. I swallowed even though every part of me wanted to wiggle and cry out, as he slowly pushed his penis into me. He met no resistance, as I bit my bottom lip to keep from saying his name. Eventually I would say it, and he would love it but for now he urged me to be quiet. I flexed my fingers against the door to gain purchase, for something to hold on to and to ground me in the sensation or I'd come before we even started.

"You're still squirming." He pulled his belt tighter,

I swallowed as he huffed in exasperation pulling out of me, before picking me up by the waist and carrying me. He went straight into the bedroom, where I was thankful I had left the light on and tossed me on the bed. It was an ungraceful plop before he twisted my hips so I lay on my stomach, and then he secured the belt to the wrought iron bed frame.

I couldn't believe he remembered the location of my bed, from the one naughty picture I sent. Drunk and high on what grew between us, I took an awkward naked selfie that had my black-swirled bed frame in the backdrop. As he tightened the belt I wanted to ask him how he remembered, but I didn't think he was above spanking me. He'd tied me close to the bottom of the frame, but I couldn't turn around to see him. The sound of clothing hitting the floor in a soft fluff, awakened my other senses. After a moment the bed dipped near my knees, as he climbed up onto the coverlet. He pressed my legs together, and straddled them from behind.

He lay his chest down it aligned along my back, before guiding himself between my legs. I opened them slightly, so he would find my opening easier. It was like we were made for this moment, his moan of appreciation shot through me like fireworks as he slid all the way inside.

"I'm sorry, babe, but this is going to be quick. I can't control myself around you." I bit my lip to keep quiet, but he laughed. "You can answer."

"I'll probably come as soon as you start moving." I wiggled my hips up against him for good measure.

He swatted the side of my butt, and balanced his weight on his side to help him ease in and out of me. It started slow, and I wanted to rage against my bindings to make him go faster.

"Please," I whimpered.

He pushed in a little faster, but still slow, his hot flesh was smooth against my own as he moved.

"Please what?"

"Please just fuck me."

"All you had to do was ask."

He took off, and pulled my hips so my knees supported my weight. It was an incredibly awkward position because I didn't quite get it at first, but he pressed the top half of my body into the bed and I supported my weight at my elbow while he maneuvered to slide back inside of me.

"I won't be easy," he said in a smoky voice.

"Then don't."

He pressed gently, but his grip on my hips belie his restraint.

"Say it again," he whispered.

I raised my voice above a whisper.

"Fuck me."

"Louder."

I yelled this time.

"Fuck me."

"Yes ma'am."

He didn't need to be told again, rearing his hips back almost pulling all the way out of me before sliding back in. It wasn't a forceful slam into me, but a controlled glide all the way to my core. I wasn't going to last like this.

He reached around and pressed two fingers into my clit, as he continued his brutal pace. All he did was hold them there, my body maneuvering around them to press against the perfect amount of sensation right where I needed it. Just as my fingers started to tingle with the telltale sign of impending numbness, my orgasm built.

"You're going to come, aren't you?" he asked increasing his already fast tempo. "I'm going to come with you. Wait for me."

I didn't think I could, but he rocked his hips into me and increased the pressure of his fingers. I broke apart, just as I felt the first spasm of him against my ass. He pumped once more, resting his hips against my ass cheeks as I tumbled down off a cliff I didn't know existed. Dots danced in my vision, and my knees gave out. We ended in a tumble, him sprawled across my back.

He unfastened the loop securing my hands.

"Hold on, babe."

After he released me, he rubbed from my wrists across my palms and into my fingers until all the sensation returned. He weighed a lot, but it was a comforting weight and I didn't mind it.

When he rolled off me, I almost objected until he rolled me over into the crook of his arm. I lay on his chest, running my hand down his chest onto his belly.

A fine dusting of hair marked the path down his torso.

"Was it what you expected?" he asked, as he brought my fingers to his lips and kissed the tips.

The waves of my orgasm still flowed through me with every heartbeat, and I knew nothing I had imagined would compare to this.

"No, it was better."

Home Depot Raunch
By Rafaelito V. Sy

Dear Derek,

So you finally call me, and when you do, I'm the wrong number. You think I'm a piece of shit that you can dick around like that? I opened my home to you and offered you my bed, or have you forgotten? Forgotten that night when I left my front door unlocked for you? I was in bed, you walked into my room and got on top of me without saying a word, not even "Hey." You flung your baseball cap to the floor, then eased my underwear off, as the distant ringing of a cable car bell sounded through the open window. The curtains flapped in the wind, I shivered from the cold. You tightened your arms around me, pressed your body against mine and suddenly, we were both.

Now you treat me this way.

Have you forgotten that scorching May afternoon in the park in front of my building? Kids played in the sand dune, folks sunbathed on the grass and we sat on a bench. We were stoned, sweaty, shirtless and reeked of each other's sex. A couple nearby commented to each other that the heat was indicative of an impending earthquake, so I said to you,

"If an earthquake struck and trapped me beneath a mountain of rubble, everything would be okay so long as you were with me."

You hooked your arm around my neck, my head on your heart.

"Me, too," you said.

Listen, Derek. I may be half your size, but that doesn't make me half your match. I want to punch you, slam you against a wall and tell you to your face that you're a low-life fuckhead. I want to hurt you, I want to hate you.

But I can't.

You know what I really want is for you to wrap your hand around my neck with loving hands and kiss me. Kiss me long and hard, that is all I have ever wanted. I know a kiss is what you want from me, too. Never mind that I'm from across the Pacific, a newbie to your country, a newly minted citizen of this land of the free and land of the brave. What we have between us surpasses all cultural divides. Do I dare call it the "L" word?

So don't treat me this way.

Your one and only,
Raf

The afternoon I sent you that e-mail, I didn't hear back from you. I checked my e-mail messages that night, all day at work the next day and the day after. I had not intended to communicate with you again. Five months earlier, we ran into each other at the Berkeley Steamworks. I walked into your room and touched you. You had pushed my hand away, and told me that you needed a moment of privacy. You had not returned my calls, and were pissed at me because I broke the golden rule of our tryst: I sent you a birthday card, which your boyfriend read. In it I had written,

To my special buddy.

Enjoy your special day and thanks always for the special moments we share.

The rule was no communication other than e-mails and text messages. If phone calls were involved, it would be you that initiated them. I was aware of the risk of sending you a card. It was a risk I was willing to take, because for once I wanted to do something from the heart. It cost me. I was resolved to never seeing or hearing from you again, until my phone rang and it was your name that popped up on my ID caller. Your name after five months, I still couldn't bring myself to get rid of your number.

"Derek," I said.

You were silent for a moment, before you said,

"Hey. I must have pressed your number by accident."

"Oh?"

"Yeah."

You still have my number, I thought.

"Anyway, take care," you said.

"You, too," I said.

I didn't intend to communicate with you again, but what the heck? I had nothing to lose.

***

A week after I sent the e-mail, my phone rang; my ID caller indicated your name again. This time I was not the wrong number. Your tone was different, not cold and stern but welcoming. The tone that once sent me soaring in anticipation of hours of no-holds-barred bonding with the most beautiful man in the world - your 5'11 frame carried 220 pounds of a rugby player's muscles; your square jawline and wavy, dark brown hair - the stuff of locker room desires.

When we met, you were moonlighting as an escort, and charged $250 an hour. With me, it was without charge. Hustling was a kinky kick for you. What's truly intoxicating about you is you have the brains to match your sleaze. A flight nurse is no dummy. A flight nurse is a special breed of paramedic who administers first-aid to airline passengers who have seizures, diabetic attacks and migraines while mid-flight. I used to imagine your lips pressed against some unconscious fellow, performing mouth-to-mouth resuscitation on a nameless and faceless person who had no place in your life. Yet to this person, you gave a part of yourself that you withheld from me.

"Kissing means my emotions are involved," you said once.

Every now and then, though, you allowed your emotions to get the best of you. You would press my gym body against yours, stroke my cheeks and peck me on the lips. A peck means nothing to most people, but with you, it meant that the door to your heart was cracked open. I had one foot inside.

"Got your e-mail," you said. "I read it several times, just read it again."

"Is all forgiven?" I asked.

"Forget about that. We'll do what you wrote in the e-mail."

The kiss?

"When?"

"This Sunday. You remember where I live?"

"What about him?"

"That's over."

***

Sunday.

You lived in a duplex on Folsom Street, which you took me to on the morning we first met two years earlier. We fucked for the first time at the Mack Folsom Prison sex club, where the club was thinned out as you walked in. You wore a leather harness, and I was naked standing by a sling. Without a word, you lifted me into the sling, and got on your knees so that your face was level with my ass. You probed my orifice with your tongue, before you stood to show off the full glory of your jock perfection. Your engorged penis poked through my ass cheeks, slid deep inside me and stimulated my rectal muscles. I was no longer man, I was a butthole on a sling. Your eyes were dark, but at the jerk of my hips, scintillated with pleasure.

"Let's go back to my place." Your salacious grin was unmistakable.

Two years later, I was at your place once again. It was morning, the curtains drawn as they had been during our first fuck. Sunlight bathed the wooden floors and white walls. The goldfish in the aquarium were specks of darting light. I looked around for you in the living room. The only parts of you I saw were your jeans, piss-stained Jockeys and black tee piled atop your sneakers. I gazed up and there you gazed down at me from the second level. Your eye color alternated between brown and blue, depending on the fall of the light. You were shirtless, muscled, proud and hungry.

"May I get naked?" I asked. It was a rhetorical question, as my shirt was halfway off.

"No."

I froze, listening to my own breathing.

"I want to do something we've never done before."

"What would that be?"

"Let's go shopping at Home Depot."

"Huh?"

"Trust me. You trust me, don't you, Raf?"

"That's why I'm here."

We got in your car, zoomed up Folsom Street, took a left on 6th and onto the 101 South freeway. You filled me in on what we would do at Home Depot. Our windows were down, but your deep voice overrode the blasting whistle of wind,

"Go to the toilet stall reserved for wheelchairs, and shut yourself in. I'll follow after, and knock on the door. You'll know it's me, because you'll recognize my sneakers underneath."

"Then what?" I asked.

"What do you think?"

"So public?"

You didn't say anything, just kept driving, accelerated the speed.

"I trust you," I said.

"That's more like it," you said, your foot on the gas pedal.

The Home Depot parking lot was full. The aisles bustled with people filling their carts with all sorts of home renovating thingamajigs. The bathroom was blinding bright from the high wattage of lights illuminating the store. Lights bounced off the white bathroom tiles, and reflected off the mirror. The sink counter was messy with water puddles, and crumpled paper towels overflowed from the trash bin littering the floor. There were three toilet stalls, my designation was the last stall and I waited there for a good ten minutes. Every time the bathroom door creaked open, I anticipated you.

Were you coming? How long do I have to be here with my pants down? When the fuck do we get started?

About four different guys took a piss before the bathroom was empty. Finally I heard your knock. The moment I let you in, you slammed the door shut, bolted it, clamped your hand over my mouth and looked into my eyes. I placed my arms around you, we faced each other silently for a long moment. With your eyes you relayed the instructions you had given me earlier, and mine gave my acquiescence.

The truth was that if you were to kiss me, I didn't want it like this. I would have wanted it tenderly, on a bed by candlelight. But that was not how you saw me. If I told you no, and walked out of the toilet stall, I would have lost you forever.

You moved your lips from my mouth. I unbuckled your jeans, slid them down to your ankles, got on my knees and licked your cock through your white briefs. Your manhood bulged and rose above the waistband, so that the tip of its head peaked out. Your skivvies were wet with my spit and your pre-cum.

Spitting on your fingers, you bent over me, and smeared it on my fuck lips. I ground my hips so that I could suck your fingers up my asshole, and groaned.

"Shh!" you hissed, ramming your penis down my throat as a mouth plug.

I slobbered over your prick, with its thick, soft mushroom head. I sucked and licked it, until it glistened with my saliva. I withdrew from your penis, so that I could have a breather. Before I could take a full breath, you turned around and shoved my face in between your bulbous ass cheeks. Your anus was moist, succulent and tender. You had an alpha male smell to you, meaty and musky.

"Goddamn, fuck yeah!" You grunted in a prayer-like whisper, because you couldn't believe that being with a man could feel so good. That having the darkest, most secret part of your body being worshiped could feel so good. God gave you a beautiful ass, and He gave me life to relish it. You shoved my face so far up inside of you that I almost suffocated. Just when I thought I was going to pass out, you turned around so that your son of a bitch cock was in front of my face and you pummeled my mouth. I looked up at you, your eyes ran the gamut of lust: hate, love, disgust and desire.

Desire.

You slid your arms against my armpits, pulled me up to my feet, twirled me around and bent me over the toilet bowl. Then you grabbed a toilet plunger, and slapped it against the wall above me. The plunger handle stuck out like a two-foot ramrod.

"You want to belong to me?" you asked.

"Yes, I do. You know I do."

"My toilet sex slave."

Your slave. Your toy. Your hole. Your lover.

You slid your cock inside me, Derek. It just slid in there, as if that was where it was meant to be like a gun in its holster.

"I'm fingering my own asshole right now," you said.

"Oh, fuck!" I moaned.

You started fucking fast. Furiously. Brutally.

"Derek, you're hurting me," I said.

No response.

"Please. Be easy. Please."

You stuffed toilet paper in my mouth, and said,

"Shut your yacking shithole."

I shut my eyes, spat out the paper and ground my teeth. You fucked with such ferocity, I swear your cock was poking my heart. You could have dick-pounded my heart out of my mouth, and still you would not have stopped. As though I weren't already enslaved to you, you tied my hands together behind my back with the toilet bib. Who knew bathroom paper could bind so strongly?

"You ain't going anywhere, slut," you said.

As if I could ever leave you, as if I ever would want to.

Somebody walked in.

The bathroom door creaked and swung open, and footsteps made their way to the urinals. You stuck your manhole fingers into my mouth, and flushed the toilet to drown out our noises.

We were in there for an eternity, fucking, sucking and eating ass. I don't know how many guys must have walked in since the first dude. Once, a dad walked in with his tot. You whispered into my ear amid the whirl of flushing water,

"Family time. In all due respect, we need to stop while dad's here."

Respect? You actually know the meaning of the word? Could have fooled me because the minute dad and tot stepped out, you rotated your hips, ground your cock up my sphincter and smothered my face with your anal-sweaty fingers so that I'd stink like your nasty ass skank.

We were in there for an eternity. Still, it wasn't enough, I broke into a sob.

"Fucking bitch, are you crying?" you asked.

"No," I said. "No."

It would not have mattered to you that I was. You had reached the brink of letting go. Your orgasm was something else, you didn't thrust hard but slowed down, became quiet and mute. My hips moved in sync with yours, the entire length of your penis slid in and out against my smooth butt walls. I discovered parts of me I had never known existed, as we were one.

One rhythm. One breath. One body.

You slammed your cock deep inside me.

Deep.

I gasped.

You unleashed your sperm, and I felt your shaft pulsate with every drop. It was like a spring inside of me, steaming my blood with hot fluid.

I gasped.

You gently held my head back, and placed your lips on mine kissing me passionately and deeply. You gorged on my tongue to savor the taste of your own asshole. We could have died in each other's arms right there, in a dingy toilet stall. With our bodies intertwined, your dick locked in the core of my physical being, our mouths joined and each of us inhaling each other's breath, it were as if we had both reached the gates of Nirvana.

But alive I am and alive you are.

On our drive back to the city, I sat naked in the passenger seat and you drove naked with my juices dripping down your balls. In your glove compartment was a butt plug, you had me shove up my fuck hole.

"Keep me in you," you ordered.

"Gladly," I said.

"How are you doing?"

"Great," I said. And I wasn't exaggerating.

I'm alive and you're alive, but we don't see each other anymore. The last time I was at your place, your books were boxed and your fish tank was empty. You were paying off bills, and changing your mailing address.

"I'm moving back to Chicago," you said.

"I see,"

Just like that, you were gone. These types of connections often end on a silent note. At times I wonder why it never worked between you and me. Guarded emotions? The enigmatic interplay of lust and love? Why get philosophical? The truth is, we never really knew each other, did we?

Yet you'll never be away from me. You're in my guts forever, fucker, as surely that I'm a sensation that will burn in your memory for the rest of your life.

I see you now, flying high in the sky in your suit and tie, holding a guy's head back and pumping his heart in order to revive him to life. You have no doubt kissed other men since me, violated many a male rectum for your manly needs and pleasure. You probably have told a man that you love him, maybe live with him and cozy up to him in front of a hearth, underneath a warm blanket.

If some other stud does happen to be by your side, kiss him without restraint. Kiss him, tell him you can't live without him and love him with all your might.

I wish the lucky fuck could be me, but our time has passed. I can live with that, you son of a bitch, because whoever your new slut might be, he'll never be able to take away the one treasure that ties me to you… forever - the memory of our Home Depot raunch.

By a Thread

By Jane Gilbert

The spool of cotton stands solemnly at the far end of the table, a rotund little soldier wrapped in snowy white. You eye it warily, your hands clasped together in your lap, and shoot me nervous glances, eyes flickering like silver min nows.

I drop my weight onto my heels and stare down from my greater height, savoring the unspoken words hanging in the no-man's land between us.

"Stand up."

You rise from the hard wooden chair, fidgeting from one foot to the other, little lines creasing the space between your eyebrows as you turn the possibilities over and over in your head.

Oh pet.

I smile, the kind curve of my lips a falsehood, a cuckoo, and slip my fingers beneath your chin, tilting it upwards. My free hand dislodges the thin straps of your sundress and I pull the bodice down so it bunches at your waist. You're fucking flat as hell, boyish almost, but your absent, braless tits are fast becoming my favorite playground – your embarrassment of them only fueling my desire to lavish attention.

I capture a deliciously fat nipple between my lips, suckling and pulling until the areola bunches, puckers, its crown forming a warm little pebble on my tongue. The low whine of frustration that gurgles from your throat when I finally remove my mouth is charming, your gaze tinged with undisguised frustration even more so.

Idly, I circle the proud, wet nub with my index finger, pinching it with the pad of thumb until your back curls and you arch into my hand, pretty as a green willow, fingers fisting involuntarily at your sides.

I release you. Run my thumb lightly over the smoothness of your barely convex breast. "Bend over the table."

You comply gratifyingly quickly, bending forward until your face comes to rest, cheek first, against the dark ebony top. Briefly, I wonder whether your compliance is borne from obedience, or the simple desire to shield your flatness.

Something to explore, perhaps.

But not today. No, today is for other things.

I nudge your legs apart with my foot before moving to pick up the reel of thread, the intensity of your gaze almost blinding as I locate the trailing end of the cotton and pull a few inches free so I can hold it to the light.

"Thin, isn't it?"

"Y-yes."

Delightful, how you manage to thread that one drawn-out word with so much trepidation and, though I don't think you realize it, curiosity.

"Yet surprisingly … resilient." I tug the length

firmly, enough to demonstrate its strength but not hard enough to snap it. "Wouldn't you say?"

"Er…"

I watch as you shuffle the puzzle pieces, rearranging them, your agile mind trying to put them in some sort of order. To lock them into place.

"Hands, please."

I snap off a good twenty inches from the reel and regard you expectantly. The look of surprise that flashes across your face, is followed immediately by one of suspicion. Can you smell the deliciously poisoned apple, my sweet girl? Taste the metallic tang of it on your tongue?

Yes. Yes, I think you can.

Warily, you stretch your arms above your head, the position accentuating the long, lean lines of your body. I take a moment to admire the picture you make against the glossy wood, before slipping the cotton beneath your wrists and tying the ends together in a simple granny knot; it's almost invisible against your creamy skin–nothing but a wisp. A thought.

Wonderfully fragile.

A strand of bright black hair trails across your temple and I tuck it, carefully, behind your ear.

"You're going to come for me," I murmur. My hand trails over your shoulder and neck. Along your exposed spine as, slowly, I move back around the table until the protrusion of your dress-covered buttocks halts my progress. "As many times as I want, for as long as I want." I gather the skirt in my hand, pulling it upwards to reveal your underwear and trace the scalloped edge of the waistband. "Until you're nothing but a cunt. *My cunt.*"

You make a sound of angry protest, stiffening beneath me, and attempt to rise up, your weight braced on your forearms..

"Lie down," I say sharply.

You heed the warning.

"You will keep your legs open for me at all times. You will do your very best not to move from this position. And every time you break this rule?" I press my growing erection against your hip, brace myself over you so I can stroke the barrel of cotton over your cheek. "I will cane you."

So still, so silent.

"And, pet?" I pause. "You *are* going to break it."

Not a single breath puffs from your soft, pink lips.

"Do you understand?"

No answer.

"I said, Do You Understand?"

A swallow, a nod–at least, as much as your position allows.

"Yes."

I press a tender kiss to the corner of your mouth.

***

Beeswax.

The scent curls, soft as a petal, from the deeply-grained wood inches from my nose. I latch onto it, the familiar smell my only surety. The only buoy in a sea of uncertainty.

My X factor.

Ridiculously, I find myself trying to remember when I last polished the table – last Saturday? The

Saturday before? but the thought fades almost as quickly, as it appears when my ears pick up the light clacking sound of something being placed beside me.

I don't dare turn my head to look, I already know what it is.

My failure, looming like The Grim Reaper.

I move my wrists, testing the give in the barely-there thread holding them together and my stomach flips as I realize just how precarious my binding is, how little give there is in the cotton. One good jerk and...

I jump as your hands press against the tender skin of my inner thighs, pushing them outwards.

The brush of your bare, shirtless shoulders.

The tickle of your soft hair.

The rough prickle of your unshaven jaw.

The feel of your tongue and lips probing at the crotch of my already damp panties, the pleasure of your exploration frustratingly dulled by the barrier of fabric.

I've lost count of the number of times I've cursed and sworn at you for placing me in bondage. But in this moment? I'd give anything to have my body's freedoms stripped and torn away.

I hold myself perfectly still, fighting the urge to push myself against your taunting mouth and increase the pressure, counting sheep, solving impossible sums, make my kissing wrists my world.

My everything.

And succeed right up until the moment you pull aside my underwear and sink three, thick fingers inside me, ripping apart my resolve as easily as a shred of thin, wet silk.

I turn my face into the table, groaning my unwanted arousal against it.

Oh, God, please, please let me stay still!

God, of course, doesn't hear me. Or refuses to. He's on your side. He always is. How could I have forgotten we're playing a game in which you hold all the cards, own every roll of the dice?

I count the seconds. Grit my teeth. Think of everything but the growing, nagging heat between my legs.

It's no use.

You turn my body against me, brand it traitor and I come in a shivering, wet rush all over your hand.

"Oh, dear pet," you whisper, as I slowly fall back into my skin.

My hands, press palms-down against the table, far further apart than they should be, the strand of thread lying dead between them.

No! No, no, no!

Fresh sweat breaks and sheens, a relentless wave, as you move behind me and hook your fingers into the waistband of my knickers, pulling them down so they hobble my knees.

"Three."

The number is my only warning.

I cry out as the cane bites into my flesh, its aftermath a comet that burns away my heart, my lungs.

My soul.

There's an endless moment, an eternity, as I flail in the pain. But then I hear your voice–firm, soothing, impossibly gentle–telling me how beautiful I am. How proud you are of me. I kick upwards, break the surface. Your faith, your praise, lifting me, carrying me all the way through to the third cruel lash.

And it's over.

Only it isn't.

You place the cane down on the table beside me, and rebind my hands.

***

There's nothing more beautiful than a post-orgasmic cunt.

Overblown.

Tender.

Impossibly sensitive.

I run my fingers through the sodden, swollen folds between your legs, coating them in slickness, before rubbing them gently against your distended clit. You whimper and try to press your legs together, to shield it from my touch.

"No."

I bring my palm down–hard–against one of the cane welts. You jump and your arms jerk dangerously, a hair's breadth from breaking the thread I've only just rebound them with. I'm not sure whether I'm pleased or disappointed.

Reluctantly, you part your thighs.

"It's sticking out like a little cock, you know." My words send you into a squirm of shame. Kneeling on the ground behind you, I blow gently on the hood before parting your labia pulling back the cloak of flesh to expose the pink kernel hidden within. "Tell me, pet. Does it feel like one?" I touch it–very, very softly–with the tip of my tongue, and am rewarded with a desperate, keening yelp. Your hips try to shy away from me, but the edge of the table prevents any sort of retreat. "Pretty, pretty little cock."

I hold you open, and using only my tongue and lash you with the lightest, the most delicate of licks. You come twice more, before the thread breaks. And this time, when I cane you, you float on the surface. Your overly-aroused body preventing you from slipping beneath the tide of pain. I wrap yet another length of thread around your wrists before undoing the fly of my jeans and pressing myself to your opening, the hot wetness seeping out of it is the most passionate of kisses against my hard flesh.

The sound of your sobbing as I slide inside you rivals that of an angel.

***

Crying.

Plump, salty, sweet tears.

Drip, drip, dripping down my cheeks as you ride me tenderly, relentlessly – ruthlessly –towards the dark, pendulous black cloud I can feel growing stronger and angrier with every calculated stroke of your penis. With every sly rub of your finger against the poor, tortured knot of nerves jutting between my legs.

You're the devil, whispering in my ear. Telling me how good, how perfect, I feel to you. Just how wet I am. Telling me to come. Just to come.

I shout angrily through my sobs, my skin singing a song of pain as your hand slaps against the welts scorching my buttocks.

"Go on," you croon, your voice low. Predatory. "You know you want to."

I bear down, trying to push you from my body, and immediately tighten in contrition. The urge to follow your order at war, with my equally strong desire not to give in. Not to stumble.

I can't.

Your hand tightens in my hair, and my scalp screams in protest even as the pain triggers a pulse of slickness around your swelling penis.

"My, my pet. Such spirit."

Your words only throw more gasoline on the flame of my determination.

We grapple for the upper hand.

Bend.

The increasingly frantic beat of my heart hammers a tattoo in my ears and, all of a sudden, you let go of my hair. My head lolls forward in relief.

Have…Have I…?

Break.

Pain. Deep, dense explodes from my nipple, the discomfort of it running headlong into the throbbing in my clit and the hunger in my pussy. I climax, violently, screaming your name, pressing my forehead to the table and shoving my hips back against you. Nothing more than a bitch in heat, nothing more than the cunt you promised me I would be.

You hold yourself still as I shake against the wood, overloaded, my body a wall of white inside and out. Everything I am is centered between my hollow, trembling legs.

Time ticks by. Seconds? Minutes? A lifetime? I have no idea. There's only a sudden awareness of you breathing raggedly in the quiet. Your still-hard cock throbbing inside my spent body.

Why…why didn't you come?

"Break it." Your voice is calm, as it always is, but I can hear the underlying strain. The rawness.

Break what? I don't understand. I shift slightly, feel the vague press of the cotton circling my wrists.

Oh, my God.

By some miracle, it's still intact.

Unbroken.

"Your choice, pet." You reach over my back, the movement pressing your sweat-covered chest against my spine, your penis deeper within me and I contract involuntarily around it, eliciting a pained growl. "You've earned it. We can stop right here. Or…" Your hand closes around the cane lying on the table beside me. " …we can keep going. It's entirely up to you."

Just like that, the puzzle pieces fall. Realign, reassemble. Failure…triumph… How thin that line between them is.

I pull my wrists apart, sending the severed ends of the cotton to rest against the tabletop. "Three," I say quietly. "Three."

He pulls himself from my body.

And makes every single one of them count.

I set the cane down. Run my hand over the pink lines I've called forth, gently probing the furrows before parting your buttocks and exposing the little pucker between them. Sink once into the oily well below, before pressing the head of my cock against it.

We both shout as the muscle gives, your body's juices just enough to ease my way, but not quite enough to stop the hurt. I press soft kisses to your back as I work myself inside, holding myself absolutely still when my balls finally come to brush against your cunt.

You quiver all around me, the hottest, most tender of sanctuaries.

"I love you," you whisper.

It's all I need to hear.

I let go. Feel my release flooding deep inside you.

And, ever so gently, begin to move.

True Calling
By Janie James

It all started with a bet and a book.

All Tied Up: Naughty Tales of BDSM & Bondage.

Gina had come across it at Sinfully Tasteful, the adult store across the street from the mall. Not a place she frequented that often, but she'd been put on the spot by Mark.

"I won the bet fair and square. So, my wish is for you to figure out something new and exciting to do in bed this weekend."

Betting on things was a game they'd played ever since Kyle was born. It had started out simple. Winner got to skip diaper duty for a night. Or sleep through a morning feeding. They'd both quickly realized how nice it was to win, so they'd expanded the list of things they bet on, from the Jets and Giants on Sundays to anything they could think of. Baseball games. The Oscars. The Grammys. With so many things to bet on, over time wins and losses averaged out. And when little Farrah came along, they'd gone bet-crazy. How many weeks Mark's sister would last with her latest boyfriend. Which uncle would open the first beer on Thanksgiving.

It got to the point where the betting continued even after the diaper days of their children were long gone. It had been Mark's idea to use the bets for things other than cooking dinner, doing the wash, or cleaning the garage.

In other words, for sex.

Over the years, he'd cashed in his winnings for blowjobs, hand jobs, and, once, sex on the balcony of a cruise ship. Most of the time, Gina didn't mind. It either got her out of sex when she was tired, or it led to sex, like on the cruise. And when she won, she took just as much advantage, demanding things like hot oil massages and breakfast in bed.

Still, Mark had surprised her this time.

She knew why he'd come up with such a crazy idea; the kids were gone for the weekend, visiting Mark's parents upstate. She'd expected him to request sex on Friday and Saturday, maybe even Sunday morning.

Something new and exciting for the bedroom, though? How was she supposed to do that? They'd been married twelve years; pretty much anything they could think of they'd already done.

Watch porn together? Check.

Have him pretend to pick her up in a bar? Check.

Role play? Check. And never again. That maid's outfit had itched something terrible.

In the end, she'd decided that her only option was to get a new vibrator and let him use it on her. Not exactly the kind of thing he'd probably expected, but the best she could do on short notice. So, after he'd gone to work, she'd driven to the one adult toy store in town.

That's when she'd found the book.

Bondage. That's something we've never tried.

Of course, it was something neither of them had ever shown an interest in, either. Not when talking about their fantasies, not when watching porn. Even at that moment, thinking about being tied up – or tying Mark up – seemed like a lot of trouble, and for what? You still had to have sex to get off. Gina knew there were people who enjoyed pain with their pleasure, but she'd never been one of them. A little light spanking, some hair pulling, sure, but that was it. Some of the things she'd seen people do in movies made her cringe. Nipple clamps? Leather masks that barely let you breath? Riding crops?

No thank you!

Still, she had to bring something home. She looked at the rest of the display. Fuzzy handcuffs, bonds you could attach to the bedposts, tickling feathers... it all seemed harmless enough. And better than another vibrator or a scratchy outfit.

He wants something new? I'll give him new.

Unaware she was smiling, Gina began selecting the tools of her revenge.

She couldn't wait to see his face when he came home.

***

"Gina?"

"In the bedroom." Gina's heart fluttered as she listened to Mark's footsteps on the stairs. She knew he must be getting excited, too. She'd prepared the whole house to let him know something special was waiting for him. The lights dimmed low, candles burning in every room. She'd even texted him a message saying dinner would be late because he had to collect his winnings.

But what would he think when he entered the bedroom?

Then there was no time to worry, as his silhouette appeared in the doorway.

"Honey? Are you in here?"

"Sit down," she said, doing her best to sound forceful. To her surprise, he did as he was told. After a slight hesitation, she approached him from behind and tied a black cloth around his eyes.

"What are you--?"

"Quiet, slave. Your duty is to obey orders, not question them." The lines, which she'd gotten from a story in the *Tie Me Up* book, sounded so silly she had to bite her lip to keep from laughing.

"Oh, I get it. Role playing. How come you get to be—ow!"

His exclamation came when Gina smacked his arm with the riding crop. She waited for him to make an angry comment, and when he didn't, she continued with the script she'd mentally prepared.

"Stand up and take off your clothes."

Still rubbing his arm, he got up and undid his pants, let them slide to the ground. His shirt followed, and then his shoes and socks. Even in the dim light of just two candles, she saw his erection bulging in his boxers, and a sudden urge raced through her. She tapped his balls very lightly with the crop, surprising herself by enjoying the way he jumped.

"Underwear, too, Let's go, slave."

Mark quickly pulled his boxers off and then he was standing there, his cock sticking out and up. He wore a big smile, and Gina felt a sudden annoyance. What was he expecting, her to drop to her knees and suck him?

Sorry, mister, that's not how this game is played.

"Lie down on the bed. Arms out." She raised her voice when he hesitated. "Now!"

The moment he was in position, she hurriedly wrapped the heavy mesh restraints around his wrists and then to the bedposts. The second set went around his ankles and then through around the posts on the footboard.

"Hey! What the hell? This isn't my idea of sexy."

"You asked for something different, now you have to go along with it." Gina tickled his chest and stomach with the tassels on the crop's handle. "Who knows, you might like it."

Mark opened his mouth to say something and Gina placed her hand over it.

"I said, no talking, slave. I guess we'll have to gag you." With that, she slipped the strap of the breathable gag over his head and placed the rubber ball in his mouth.

"Relax, Mark," she said, using her normal voice. "It's got a hole in it so you can breathe." Then she switched back to her role of dominatrix.

"Now you shall experience pleasure and pain, slave. If you obey me, there will be more pleasure." She stroked her fingers softly down his belly and across his now semi-hard dick, which twitched in response.

"But if you disobey..." She slapped his thigh with the crop and he cried out behind his gag.

"That's a good boy." Gina stood back and eyed her husband. Where to start? The stories in the book had all been about dominants and submissives, people who enjoyed giving and receiving pain as part of their sex lives, or even without sex. But there'd been nothing in there about what to do the first time. And she'd never expected Mark to let things go this far.

Guess I'll have to wing it.

Taking one of the candles, one designed for erotic foreplay, she ever so slowly tilted it over Mark's stomach until a few dribbles of liquid wax fell onto his skin. She'd already tested it on herself, just to make sure there was no chance of burning him. It had actually felt rather good.

He moaned and tried to pull away, and she reacted on instinct, slapping him again with the crop. This time he yelled.

"Stop being a baby. The wax isn't that hot. It can't hurt you. But it can drive you crazy not knowing where it will land next."

As she finished her sentence, she dripped a little more on his chest, right between his nipples. He jerked, but didn't make any noise.

In the candle's glow, she saw his nipples harden and the tiny hairs on his belly stand up. And they weren't the only things rising to attention. His cock had regained its former stature.

He can't be hating it that much. Smiling, she tipped the candle over his right thigh, and then his left. The scented wax poured out in a thin stream that quickly hardened. This time, he moaned and his legs shuddered. The scent of peaches filled the air. His cock spasmed.

A warm, tingling feeling came to life between Gina's legs.

She poured more wax over his thighs. Some of it ran down the curve of his muscle and touched the wrinkled flesh of his balls, causing him to moan again.

Gina put the candle down and carefully took an ice cube from the wine chiller she'd placed next to the nightstand. Holding it between two fingers, she touched one end to Mark's engorged penis.

This time he reacted the way she'd expected, violently convulsing on the bed and shouting into his gag. The words came out garbled – *"Whmph a fck aooing?"* – but she understood them just fine: *"What the fuck are you doing?"*

"Just teasing, love. You know I wouldn't hurt Mister Happy." With that, she wrapped her hand around his dick, with the ice cube still in her palm. He cried out again, and pulled at the bindings. She let her hand slide up and down his dick, while her other hand found its way down her pants to her own pleasure zone, caressing and rubbing in time to her cock stroking. Mark's objections gave way to groans, and he arched his back as she ran her frigid hand up and down his pole. She could almost taste his frustration when she let go and the ice dropped onto his balls.

"Not yet, slave. We're just getting started."

Regretfully, she stopped playing with herself so she could remove her own clothes. Shirt, pants, and bra she tossed into a far corner of the room; her panties she rubbed against herself until they were wet with her juices. Then she rubbed them under Mark's nose, leaving a glistening trail across his upper lip.

"Smell that? I'm wet. So very, very wet. I need to

be fucked. But I don't want to come right away. I want it to last a long, long time. Can you do that, slave? Can you last as long as me?"

"Ymph. Mph hmph."

"I hope so. Because if you don't..." She slid one of her vibrators between his legs, pushing it forward until the head pressed against his asshole. "Your punishment is going to be long and hard."

Gina climbed onto the bed and straddled him, lowering herself until the tip of his cock just touched her lips.

"Are you ready?" Without waiting for an answer, she dropped onto him, taking his full length inside her.

Mark made a sound between a moan and growl, and bucked his hips up against her just as she leaned forward. The sudden pressure against her clit, combined with her enflamed ardor, brought her to a fast and unexpected climax. She dug her nails into his chest as her body trembled and her thighs tightened around his. A brief but intense wave of pleasure rose up through her body and then receded. Rather than leaving her weak and spent, it filled her with energy, and she began to fuck him like a crazed beast, lifting her ass so she could slam her pussy down, each thrust ending with a grinding motion. Wet slapping noises filled the bedroom and for a few moments she felt as if she was the one with the cock, driving it home again and again. Beneath her, Mark pushed upward in time to her movements, his back arching and his ass rising up.

"That's it, slave! Fuck me! Pound me with the cock!" She raked her nails across his chest and down his sides. One hand brushed against the crop, and she picked it up and smacked his leg with it, like a jockey on a thoroughbred.

"Fuck me! Fuck me hard!" She was screaming it now, lost to her passion, unaware of anything except the sensation of his dick inside her.

Each time she came down, she felt the thrumming of the vibrator against the sensitive spot between her asshole and her pussy. She reached back and pushed the vibrator harder against Mark's ass. He shouted something and twisted beneath her. His fingers gripped the sheets and his knees bent, forcing her forward so her clit rubbed even harder against his pelvis.

The rubbing, combined with the vibrations running through her, sent her over the edge and she came again, not a wave this time but a whole series of them, like someone had plugged her into a live electrical socket. Her body went rigid and she felt her cunt tightening around Mark's cock, squeezing it like a velvet vice.

Mark pushed against her once more and then shouted something that came out as

"Ooooaamgh!"

His body stayed frozen, his ass completely off the bed, pressed against her as he finally lost control and erupted inside her, coming in hot spurts that she felt even through her own liquids that were running out and down. Again and again he released himself, until she thought he'd never stop. When he finally relaxed and pulled away, it was like a switch turning off her own orgasm and her body went limp. She fell to one side, sliding off his still-hard dick with a wet, gooey *pop!* Freed from the prison of her pussy, his cock looked like a tall, thin volcano with clearish-white lava flowing down the sides.

Gina lay still for a minute, her chest heaving and her heart pounding so hard her pulse was a deafening drumbeat in her ears. Gradually she calmed and became aware that Mark was staring at her, making *"mmph-mmph"* noises that she guessed meant he wanted to be released.

"Not yet, my love slave," she whispered. She didn't yet have the strength to speak in a normal voice. "Our night is just beginning. You're lucky I came before you, or I'd be using this right now." She pushed on the vibrator, which still rested between his thighs. He shook his head, and Gina laughed.

"You know, I'm really starting to enjoy this. I'm going to pour myself a drink, and then we'll begin round two."

She rubbed the vibrator up and down the shaft of his now half-erect dick, making it twitch.

"I wonder if I can fit both of you inside me?"

***

Two months after a simple book caught her eye in the store, Gina wondered how she'd ever been happy living a vanilla existence. It was as if opening herself to the world of bondage and discipline had done more than release a hidden sexuality; it had unlocked a whole new world for her to see.

After their first night as Master and Slave, neither she nor Mark had ever looked back. She'd spent the rest of the weekend imposing her will on him in various ways: tying him to the bed, handcuffing him to a door, walking him through the house on a leash. Somewhere along the way, their actions had morphed from role playing to a new kind of relationship, one where Gina ruled with an iron fist and Mark bowed to her wishes. She'd gagged him, strapped a studded leather cock ring around his dick, pinched and pulled at the loose skin of his testicles until he begged her to stop, attached tiny clamps to his nipples, and violated his ass with a new toy she'd picked up, a vibrating oval "egg" on a cord.

She'd also fucked him in every position possible where a woman could control the action. On top, reverse cowboy, scissor. Suddenly insatiable, she'd purposely only let him come once each day, so that he'd always be anxious and horny and ready to please her. And when he was too worn out to get it up, she'd pinned him to the bed and ground her pussy into his face or whipped him with her crop while he use one – and sometimes two – vibrators on her.

By the time Sunday came, Gina was so sore she could barely walk, and Mark wore dozens of welts on his arms, legs, and chest, which matched the red, bruised skin of his cock.

After putting the kids to bed on Sunday, he climbed under the covers and fell instantly asleep. Gina had worried that their lives would return to the lifeless routine they'd been in before, with only their bets providing opportunities for her to indulge in her newfound lust for control.

Monday morning, she woke to find Mark kneeling by her side of the bed.

"How can I serve you today, Master?"

At that moment, she knew her life would never be the same.

***

For a while, having Mark as her slave was enough for Gina. They made sure to act the same as always in front of Kyle and Farrah, who, at nine and seven respectively, were old enough to notice if Mommy suddenly started ordering Daddy around. But once the kids were asleep, or left behind with a babysitter, then Gina took charge. Although they never discussed why taking on their dominant and submissive roles pleased them so much, Gina suspected it was because she'd been raised in a family where the women catered to the men. For Mark, she suspected it was the pressure of running a successful law office, one that required him to constantly tell people what to do, where his was his desk that the buck always stopped at. When he got home, he didn't want to be in charge; he simply wanted to be told what to do.

Except eventually it wasn't enough. Not for Gina. She yearned to command him at all times. She also had her new sex drive to contend with, an unquenchable desire to impale herself on a thick, hard cock while she inflicted just enough pain to make her partner squirm.

That was when she broke down and began searching the 'net for ways to release her wanton desires without cheating on her husband.

The web provided a wealth of possibilities, but nothing that seemed to match her needs.

Sites like Alternative.com, The Wild Ones, Dungeons and Delights, OnYourKnees.com, and others offered willing partners for lust-filled affairs, but the idea of doing things behind Mark's back – or while he was at work – made her feel guilty.

There were S&M and BDSM clubs, some of them close to their house. Paddles. Bad Boys & Girls Club. The Basement. Leather and Leather. They sounded interesting, and she made a note to check them out the next time the kids were away. But again, she couldn't picture herself visiting them on her own.

Even Craigslist had an entire section devoted to BDSM ads, with headlines such as *Seeking BDSM Top M4F, Bottom Seeking Experienced Top M4F or M, Leather & Lace Party This Saturday!, and Submissive male seeks dom female for weekend fun.*

But that went back to the whole cheating thing, a road she had no intention of going down.

And then one afternoon, she came across an ad:

Wanted: Dominatrix. Will Train. No Sex.

Fem-Dom now hiring.

Below it was a number.

Gina stared at the screen for long while before dialing. The voice that answered was rough and throaty, like a lioness that had learned to speak.

"Hello, Fem-Dom. Lady Escalade speaking."

Suddenly self-conscious, Gina stammered out her words. "Hi, um, I'm calling about the ad for a dominatrix?"

"Do you have experience?"

"Well, I've been dominating my husband for about two months. You know, I tie him up, make him wear a collar, sometimes I whip him. Only when we're alone, of course."

"Of course, sweetheart. Wouldn't want the kiddies to see, and all that. When can you come down for a try-out?"

"Um, try-out? The ad says no sex."

"Not that kind of try-out. But you can have sex if you want. We just have to say that 'cause you can't charge for sex, right? You're not a cop are you?" The voice grew suspicious.

"No! But, I can't do the sex. My husband... that would be cheating."

"Honey, I though you said you were a dom. It's not cheating if you tell him you're doing it. Hell, you can bring him down and tie him up so he has to watch."

A warm, tingling feeling came to life between Gina's legs. *That's true. I'm the one in charge of sex around here. Mark has to do what I say, or suffer his punishment.*

"I'll be there in an hour."

Gina slipped the leather mask over Mark's head and pulled the zipper shut, leaving only his eyes and nose exposed. Nervousness warred with a hot, aching yearning inside her as she checked the cotton-wrapped manacles holding him in place against the wall. Naked except for a leather bikini underwear with the crotch cut out, he was ripe and ready for his punishment.

"You've been a bad, bad, boy," she said, running her new, red-leather crop up the inside of one thigh, across his balls, and down the other thigh. His dick thickened at her touch, growing longer as blood rushed to it.

After taking the job at Fem-Dom, Gina had worked three day shifts to make sure it was right for her before telling Mark. As it turned out, the job was everything she could have hoped for and more. She could see four or five clients between the hours of 10:00 and 2:00, and still be back at the house before the kids got home from school, with a nice $600 cash in her pocket.

Plus, she'd given her pussy a nice workout on two of those days, once with a young stud who needed his ass whipped before he could get hard, and once with an older black gentleman who had the hugest cock she'd ever seen, so big she'd just had to ride it, despite not being attracted to him. Of course, she'd made him lick her feet and plead for her pussy, and even then only mounted him after spanking him with a paddle and walking him through the halls like a dog. She'd been so hot and wet by that point that she'd taken his entire length without any problem, and come almost instantly just from the thought of it being inside her.

At that point, she'd known she simply couldn't turn down the job. It was perfect. So that night, after the kids were in bed, she'd told Mark what she'd done.

And he'd objected. Told her "No wife of mine is going to work in a place like that."

So she'd ordered him to roll over and put his hands behind his back. She'd handcuffed him that way, using the real ones she'd brought home, not the comfy, fuzz-covered toy cuffs. She'd clamped them tight, tight enough to leave marks so that he'd have to wear long sleeves to work the next two days. Made him lay like that while she masturbated with a thick, black dildo and re-enacted what she'd done with her client earlier that day. She'd done it all without guilt.

Because she'd seen the gleam in his eye when he tried to assert his manhood. The look that told her he wanted to be punished. Needed it.

So he'd gotten it. But Gina wasn't done. Being a

slave meant total obedience. And so she'd devised a second part to his punishment.

He would experience what her clients experienced.

She'd arranged a special session for Mark, at the hands of Lady Escalade herself, the owner of Fem-Dom.

"Bad boys need discipline. Do you need discipline, slave?"

Mark nodded, his eyes alight at the thought of the penalty his wife would be inflicting on him.

Instead, Gina turned to a hidden window, one of many disguised portals put in place to ensure the safety of clients and doms alike.

"We're ready."

Black curtains parted and Lady Escalade entered, her full-figured body wrapped in a studded leather corset, her muscular legs fitted into thigh-high black leather stiletto boots. She wore a satin mask over her eyes and had her raven-black hair pulled up in a tower. With one hand, she led Gina's giant-cocked client by a chain leash attached by clips to his nipples. In her other hand she carried a miniature cat o-nine tails, a wooden rod with nine thin leather strips dangling from the end.

"Step forward slave," Gina said to Mark, who moved away from the wall as far as his manacles allowed. It left just enough room between him and the wall for Lady Escalade to step behind him. He tried to turn his head to see what she was doing, but the mask blocked his view. He returned his gaze to Gina, who ordered her client to get on his hands and knees.

"This is how we deal with disobedient slaves." Gina brought her crop down across the client's ass with a resounding *smack!* He let out a gasp. She struck him again, this time leaving a welt across his dark skin. She landed a third blow on his other ass cheek, and he cried out.

"Silence!" Gina stepped on his hand, using just enough pressure with the toe of her boot to create discomfort. The client moaned. Keeping her foot in place, she reached down with the crop and tapped it against his dangling ball sack. Each tap drew a whimper from the client, and tears ran down his cheeks.

"Turn over," she ordered him. He complied, lying down on his back. His engorged cock rose up like an ebony tower, thick as Gina's wrist and longer than anything she'd ever seen in a movie.

"Do you see that?" she said to Mark, pointing at the massive phallus. "I am going to put that inside me. You are going to watch. And while you do, you'll take your punishment like a good slave."

On cue, Lady Escalade struck her whips across Mark's ass. He shouted, more in surprise than pain, his cry muffled by the leather.

Gina slipped a condom onto the client's dick and poised herself above the quivering rod. She lowered herself down, savoring every fat inch as it slid into her, the ridges of flesh igniting wave after wave of passion in her cunt until her fluids ran out like a river.

Lady Escalade swung her arm back and forth, lashing Mark's shoulder, back, and ass with the whips, using just enough force to redden flesh without breaking the skin. In between strokes, she reached between his legs and fondled his cock and balls, alternating between delivering pain and pleasure.

Throughout it all, Gina kept her gaze on Mark.

And in her husband's eyes, saw nothing but love.

Electric sensations exploded inside her, and she screamed as her first orgasm of the afternoon ravaged her body. At the height of it, Lady Escalade gripped Mark's dick and he came as well, shooting white streams across the floor and onto the client's arm.

After recovering her breath, Gina gave Mark her sternest expression.

"What are you?" she asked.

"I am your slave," he said, and she understood him despite his mask.

"And who am I?"

"My master."

"Very good." She smiled and licked her lips. "Now watch your master carefully. Because when I'm done, it's your turn."

As she ground herself against her client, Gina couldn't help but wonder at the strange turns life could take.

If not for a bet and a book, she'd never have found her true calling.

About the Authors

Del Carmen is a sexy Latina from the Big Apple. Her work has been published by Ravenous Romance and Cleis Press, and has appeared in *Star, Penthouse* and *Cosmopolitan* for Latina magazines. Visit her at www.mydelcarmen.com.

Monica Corwin is an outspoken writer who attempts to make romance accessible to everyone no matter their preferences. As a new Northern Ohioian, Monica enjoys snowdrifts, three seasons of weather and disliking Michigan. When not writing, Monica spends time with her daughter and her ever-growing collection of tomes about King Arthur. You can find Monica Corwin on the web at www.monicacorwin.com, twitter.com/monica_corwin, and www.facebook.com/monicacorwin.

Mercedes Cruz is a Latina living and writing in New York City. Her short stories include multicultural characters living within the five boroughs. She is currently working on her first novella. Mercedes was inspired by both Telenovelas, and stories she heard as a young woman growing up. All of the above, coupled with her love of the state of New York and the arts, are often showcased in her stories.

A Kiwi-Brit hybrid, **Jane Gilbert** has an accent that confuses her friends, her neighbors and her children. She writes BDSM-themed erotica from behind her floral curtains, and blogs about kinky, sexy things at www.behindthechintzcurtain.com.

Tomio Hall-Black is a submissive man in a total power release relationship with the woman of his dreams, Delila Black. He blogs infrequently at Masculine Submission (http://www.masculine submission.wordpress.com) and at For the Love of Dominance (http://fortheloveofdominance.blogspot. com). He owns and co-moderates the Fetlife group "Submissive Men and the Women Who Love Them" as a community resource for those who are interested in female domination and/or male submission. He has self-published multiple volumes of erotic short stories focused on female domination, and has contributed to several print anthologies.

Daily Hollow is an erotic romance writer residing in the Carolinas. He is married, has a young son, three dogs, two rats and a cat. He has had two stories published in the *Tie Me Up* and *My Kinky Valentine* anthologies. His recently released story, *Eve's Daisy*, spent about a week in Amazon's top 100 and Amazon UK's top 20. He is currently working on his second novel, *The Covens*, which he hopes to have published by mid-summer. In his free time he likes to read, walk, workout, spend time with his family and flirt with the lovely women at Hot BBR. His Facebook page is: https://www.facebook.com/profile.php?id=100006816 585303.

Janie James is a former scientist with a lust for love and life. After years of toiling in laboratories and photographing crime scenes, she gave up the 9-to-5 routine to write erotic fiction. When she's not writing, she enjoys sleeping late, overdosing on coffee and watching online porn.

For more information about Janie James and her books, visit www.amazon.com/author/janiejames www.facebook.com/thejaniejames www.twitter.com/thejaniejames.

Cheryl Kaye is a British sex blogger and writer based in the Midlands. She's currently studying a postgraduate qualification in writing. She started writing erotica as part of her journey to re-find herself, and she found her home. This is her first published work. You can find Cheryl online as HornyGeekGirl at www.hornygeekgirl.com

Tabitha Kitten is an English author of erotica short stories. Her stories are published in *The Intimate Stranger and other Erotic Stories*; *Do Not Disturb*: *an Erotica Collection*; *The Mammoth Book of Urban Erotic Confessions*; *Flappers, Jazz and Valentino and Stacked.*

Annabeth Leong wears high heels and frequents the former haunts of H.P. Lovecraft. One month, she is a baseball fanatic, and the next she's reading about squid. She is frequently confused about her sexuality, but enjoys searching for answers. Her work appears in more than 40 anthologies, including *Best Bondage Erotica* 2013, 2014, and 2015, *Best Erotic Romance*

2014 and 2015, and *Best Women's Erotica* 2015. Her latest erotic novel is *Untouched*, from Sweetmeats Press. Find Annabeth online at www.annabeth erotica.com, and on Twitter @AnnabethLeong.

Born and raised in New York, **Vita Perez** lives and works out of her apartment in Brooklyn. A lover of art and self-professed romance junkie, she spends her free time, when not writing, reading and visiting galleries throughout the city. She is a true believer in love at first sight, and that the best stories come when opposites attract and sparks fly. She seeks to create stories of love and romance that reflect the people and the world around her. Vita is currently working on her first full-length novel. Visit www.VitaPerez Writes.blogspot.com, e-mail her vitawritesromance @gmail.com or follow her Twitter @VitaPerezWrites.

Oleander Plume writes erotica in her sleep, (and occasionally while she's awake). While her favorite genre is gay romance, she occasionally dabbles in other erotic flavors. Want another taste? Please visit http://poisonpendirtymind.com for sexy stories, essays about sex & writing, and more.

Marie Rebelle has self-published two books both under different pen names, one of them was erotic fiction. She has also been published in the following anthologies: *Seks, Genot en Grenzen: Fisten of Vuistneuken* (Dutch), *Southbank Seduction* and *The Big Book of Submission*.

You can find Marie on Rebel's Notes (www. rebelsnotes.com), Wicked Wednesday (www.wicked

wednesday.rebelsnotes.com), Marie Rebelle's Projects (www.365.rebelsnotes.com), as well as Twitter (https://twitter.com/RebelsNotes), Facebook (www. facebook.com/marie.rebelle.79) and LinkedIn (www. linkedin.com/in/marierebelle).

Kaysee Renee Robichaud is the author of sizzling, romantic fiction found in such anthologies as *Seductress*, *Only in the City*, *Sense and Sensuality*, *Wildfires*, *Like a Cunning Plan* and *Geek Lust*. Kaysee also writes as C. C. Blake, author of the supernatural and dark suspense thrillers *Cave and the Vamp*, *Divinest Sense*, *Kane and the Hungry Dead*, *The Go-To Girl* and *The Murder Cage*.

Rafaelito V. Sy is from Manila, Philippines. His first novel, *Potato Queen*, came out in 2005. It explores the relationships between gay Anglos and Asians in 1990s San Francisco. His erotica has also appeared in *Best Gay Erotica* 2012, *Steam Bath*, and *Pledges* anthologies. Visit his blog at www.rafsy.com, where writes about films and other creative works that inspire him.

Vanessa Clark writes lesbian, gay, bisexual, intersex, and trans romance/erotica fiction that she affectionately calls "glitterotica." After having numerous short erotica stories published on Oysters&Chocolate.com, she has since had various erotic shorts published in anthologies under her initials, V.C. She has been published by O&C Press, Ravenous Romance, Freaky Fountain, Cleis Press, Go Deeper Press, House of Erotica, Robinson/Running

Press, and Wayward Ink Publishing. You can contact her at foxxy.kitty@yahoo.com and follow her on Twitter @FoxxyGlamKitty, Facebook: www.face book.com/vcerotica and her blog: http://vcerotica glitterotica.blogspot.com. for news and much more!

Salome Wilde (@salomewilde) has published dozens of erotic stories, in a variety of genres and featuring a wide array of orientations and kinks. She is editor of *Shakespearotica: Queering the Bard* and co-editor (with co-conspirator Talon Rihai) of the forthcoming *Desire Behind Bars: Lesbian Prison Erotica* (Bella). More at www.salandtalerotica.com.

The Vixen is a steamy romance writer based in New York, City and is the voice behind the provocative sex blog and pleasure boutique, My Little Vixen. When she's a not writing kinky love stories, she works as a fashion copywriter and creative work with a number of brands. Graduating in 2012 with a degree in business and global studies, she pursues her passion of being a creative entrepreneur and a writer of beautiful romance stories. Besides being a hopeless romantic writer, she enjoys traveling, cooking, and best of all, an excellent book.

For more information, please visit www.my littlevixen.com

Nicole Wilder lives in Michigan where she has plenty of experience in the snow. She has been writing romances for twenty years, and loves to share them with others. She is the author of many short stories, newspaper articles and blog posts. She has a Best

Erotic Stories Readers's Choice Award, and wrote for Adult Stars Magazine for five years.

F. Leonora Solomon is an editor and writer, and native New Yorker. As an editor, she has published several anthologies. *Tie Me Up* is her first with Riverdale Avenue Books.

As a writer, her short stories have been featured in several anthologies, including *Chemical [se]X* and *Spy Games*. Visit her at fdotleonora.wordpress.com, or find her on Facebook, Twitter, Google+ and Ello.

Look for these other books from Riverdale Avenue Books:

The First Annual BDSM Writers Con Anthology
by Lori Perkins, Dr. Charley Ferrer

http://riverdaleavebooks.com/books/5129/the-first-annual-bdsm-writers-con-anthology

Her Wish is Your Command: Twenty-One Erotic FemDom Stories
by DL King

http://riverdaleavebooks.com/books/4107/her-wish-is-your-command-twenty-one-erotic-femdom-stories

The Glass Stiletto
by Rachel Kenley

http://riverdaleavebooks.com/books/5168/the-glass-stiletto

MASTER: The Sexuality, Politics, Life and Philosophy of a Master
by Master R
http://riverdaleavebooks.com/books/22/master-the-sexuality-politics-life-and-philosophy-of-a-master

Spank Me, Mr. Darcy
by Lissa Trevor, Jane Austen
http://riverdaleavebooks.com/books/36/spank-me-mr-darcy

The Bossman
by Renee Rose
http://riverdaleavebooks.com/books/4112/the-bossman

Mob Mistress
Book Two in The Bossman Series
by Renee Rose
http://riverdaleavebooks.com/books/5155/mob-mistress-book-two-in-the-bossman-series
by Renee Rose

50 Shades of Gay
by Jeffery Self
http://riverdaleavebooks.com/books/27/50-shades-of-gay

Made in the USA
Charleston, SC
10 August 2015